SUMMER 1941

Braide Keyland

SUMMER 1941

Wabokat Publishing Co.
San Diego, California

First Edition.

Published by Wabokat Publishing Co.
Keyland Wabokat LLC, California.

Published and Printed in the United States of America

ISBN: 978-0-9664753-2-6

Library of Congress Control Number: 2022911825

Library of Congress has cataloged the Wabokat Edition as follows: Keyland, Braide
Summer 1941/Braide Keyland.

"Everything is determined, the beginning as well as the end, by forces over which we have no control...we all dance to the mysterious tune, intoned in the distance by an invisible piper."

— Albert Einstein.

1964

Chapter 1

It is said your fate is written in the stars. Drift away, it calls to you.

Boston elite and descendant of a founding father, Sarah Wescott was born into a life of opulence that only wealth could provide. With this extravagance came a grave responsibility that could not be ignored. She had been predestined since birth to honoring her family's history of tradition revered for generations. Now when she thought she could change her destiny, fate didn't grant her that luxury, but chose for her.

Sarah Wescott pushed away the heavy drape hanging across the cathedral window of the Wescott mansion. She looked out beyond the heavy iron entry gate leading to Beacon Street and across to the historic park Boston Common. Fall had come early to Boston where the air was crisp and the wind strong, a prelude to the awakening of a season of cold and barren branches.

Staring melancholy out the window, she watched the autumn leaves red and gold fall from the trees, their color heightened by the glow of the late afternoon sun. They twirled and scattered randomly as the forceful wind hurled them across the lawn, their fiery splendor rushing on to Beacon Street.

Fall was beautiful in Boston, radiating resplendent tones of the season, but not as beautiful as New York, twenty-three years ago, where it all began in the summer of 1941....

1941

Chapter 2

Glen Miller's inspirational song, *In the Mood* played softly over the intercom in New York's Saks Fifth Avenue department store in an effort to lift shoppers' spirits. War raged in Europe and no one knew if America would be drawn into the conflict.

Sarah Wescott stood at the accessory counter as shoppers bustled back and forth across the floor behind her. Removing one of her white gloves, Sarah fingered a linen handkerchief in one of the small, tissue lined boxes displayed in rows on the counter.

On the other side of the counter the saleswoman assisting Sarah, waited patiently for her customer's decision. After some careful thought, Sarah chose the one edged with Venetian lace.

"Excellent choice," said the saleswoman as she stepped closer to the counter. "Would you like it gift wrapped?"

"Yes, thank you."

"Shall I charge it to the Wescott account, madam?"

"Yes."

The saleswoman turned away to begin the gift wrapping, placing the chosen handkerchief on a table behind the counter.

As Sarah replaced her glove on her hand, the curls of

her auburn hair slightly brushed the shoulders of her blue, silk dress accented with a collar and cuffs of white linen. A blue ribbon encircled the band of her white straw hat where the brim was bent in just the right angle over her face to appear flirtatious.

Suddenly she felt uncomfortable as if someone was watching her. She turned slightly and looking across the department store floor, she noticed a tall, slender soldier in a dark blue military uniform staring at her as he leaned casually against the lingerie counter. For a moment she was mesmerized. There was something intriguing and strikingly romantic about a man in uniform. *No man looks that handsome,* she thought, finding it hard to take her eyes away.

She had never seen a soldier before, just photos, and none, she thought, looked like him, but still, there was something more. When a gentle smile formed on his face, a sudden sensation rushed through her she had never felt before. She knew nothing about him, yet it seemed as if she knew everything about him, and he didn't need to speak a word.

When she realized she too was staring she gave a quick look from side to side before determining it was on her that his eyes were clearly fixed as if he could see right through her, touching the very core of her being. She turned away to draw her attention back to the saleswoman still wrapping her gift. It wasn't proper for a young woman of twenty years, especially one of her stature and who lived a sheltered life, to accept a flirtation even if it came from a soldier.

The saleswoman returned, placing the gift wrapped in red ribbon on the counter. "May I help you with anything else, madam?" she inquired, but before Sarah could answer, Sarah heard a young man's voice beside her.

"I've never seen anything so beautiful before in my life," he said softly.

When Sarah turned to look at the face behind the voice, her eyes meeting his, the soldier said, "And no one should have eyes that blue."

Flattered, Sarah lowered her eyes and smiled.

When the saleswoman received no answer from Sarah and heard the soldier's remarks, she looked somewhat embarrassed. "I will charge your account," she said quickly, then walked away to help another customer.

"I apologize," he said. "I didn't mean to offend you in any way."

"It's alright, soldier." Sarah assured him.

"I wonder if you can help me?" he said.

"What do you mean?"

"I'm looking for a gift for my mom."

"Any one of the saleswomen can help you."

"This gift needs a special woman's touch."

Her first thought was, perhaps well dressed women went to Saks for the latest in the finest fashion, but she assumed it was a bit pricey for a soldier's pay.

"Why don't you take my purchase, soldier? I think it's a perfect gift for a mother." She lifted the package from the counter and handed to him.

"How kind of you." When he reached in his pocket to pay her, she quickly said:

"Please don't. Consider it a gift to a soldier."

"Are you sure?"

"Yes."

"Well, thank you." He stuffed the currency back in his pocket. "How would you like a cup of coffee? There's a coffee shop right across the street."

"Oh, I don't know." She wanted to very much, so why did she hesitate?

"It's the least I can do for such kindness. You wouldn't deny a soldier going off to war that simple pleasure?"

"Well..." she smiled, "...since you put it that way."

Chapter 3

The soldier removed his hat and placed it on the seat next to him. He drew his fingers through his thick, raven hair, combing it away from his forehead. As he watched Sarah remove her white gloves and set them on the table next to her handbag, a rather large diamond appeared on the ring finger of her left hand. The precious stone caught the afternoon light streaming through the coffee shop window, flashing iridescent sparkles across the table.

"So what's your name soldier?" Sarah said. "I just can't call you soldier."

"Jack. Lieutenant Jack Karsen."

"Hello Lieutenant Jack Karsen."

"Just Jack."

"Ok, just Jack," she said.

They laughed.

"I'm Sarah Wescott." She reached across the table to shake his hand. When her hand touched his, there was that sensation again, rushing through her, and she saw the look on his face as if he sensed it too.

Their hands released and fell apart when the waitress appeared at their table. "What would you like?" she said.

"Two coffees," Jack said. "I take mine black."

"Cream, no sugar," Sarah preferred.

"No sugar," the waitress confirmed and walked away.

"So tell me Jack, where are you from?" Sarah said.

"Corn country. Tallest corn you've ever seen."

"I've never seen corn growing."

"You haven't?"

She shook her head.

Suddenly a look of warmth grew in his eyes as he began to speak of home. "You stand on an old wooden porch…where spread out before you under earth's blazing blue sky are rows and rows of cornstalks as far as the eye can see…their color green heightened by the bright morning sun warming the field…and you can hear the sound of their long leaves whispering in the wind…and the corn…" he said smiling, "…pulled fresh from the stalk…sweeter than candy."

For a moment it seemed he was transported to a different place and time, standing on the old wooden porch, looking over the cornfield, the hot summer wind rising up to touch the stalks, moving across the field to find his face, rustling his hair.

"Sounds like poetry," Sarah said intrigued.

"It is…god's poetry."

"How come you know so much about corn?"

"My folks own a farm in Iowa," he said with pride in his voice.

"And you left that paradise to go fight a war?"

"You sound like my mom. She didn't want me to sign up. Twenty-two was just a boy in her mind. But Britain's in dire straits and in need of all the help it can get. Besides my brother works the farm, helping my mom since my dad died."

"What are you doing in New York?" Sarah said.

"Never been and wanted to see it. Now you know more about me than most people. Tell me about yourself?"

"Boston. Founding fathers. Steep in history. Only child. Nothing like Iowa. I would love to see Iowa someday."

The way he smiled softly at her response, it was evident the ring on her left hand meant nothing to him.

"How about a hotdog?" he said.

"Hotdog?"

"I bet you've never had a New York hotdog. Not like this one."

She found herself agreeing before she had time to think, for what harm would it do? It's just a hotdog.

Chapter 4

It was just a ten minute walk from the coffee shop to East 59th Street where Jack was told about a street vendor who sold the best hotdog in New York. On the way he and Sarah talked about New York and he marveled at the height of the buildings, fascinated by their architecture like a child who had seen a rainbow for the first time.

When they turned the corner onto East 59th Street, there was the vendor and his cart, a man in his forties wearing a blue and white striped apron. The vendor had just finished up with a couple of customers when Sarah and Jack arrived.

"Hello soldier," the vendor said cheerfully, obviously noticing the uniform. "What can I get you and your lady?"

Jack turned to Sarah. "Let's go for the works. Is that fine with you, Sarah?"

"Sure, why not?"

"Two with the works," he told the vendor and the vendor opened the steamer on his cart that held the hotdogs, stuffed two on buns and prepared to add the condiments.

"You off soon soldier, help fight the war?" the vendor said.

"Couple days," Jack said.

The vendor handed them the hotdogs wrapped tight in paper. When Jack reached in his pocket to pay for the hotdogs, the vendor placed his hand on Jack's arm and shook his head.

"Go win the war, soldier," the vendor said.

"Oh, thanks. I'm Jack Karsen." He shook the vendor's hand.

"Who's your fine young lady?" the vendor said.

"I'm Sarah." She extended her hand in a straight forward manner, indicative of an upper-class upbringing.

"I'm Harvey…" the vendor said, "…been doing this stand for ten years. Let me know what you think of the dogs?"

"I will Harvey, when I get back."

"Good luck, soldier."

Chapter 5

Jack took Sarah's hand. Together, they ran across the street from the hotdog stand to Central Park, dodging honking cars. They laughed when they reached safety and the other side.

Out of breath, she said, "Well, soldier, it seems you're already preparing for the dangers of war."

"I'm sure that's nothing like it," he said.

Sitting on a nearby bench against the backdrop of the famous Le Grand Chateau Hotel, Jack appeared to be enjoying his hotdog. Sarah took a bite of her hotdog then placed it on the seat beside her.

"You don't like the hotdog?" he said.

"Yes, I do very much. I'm just not hungry right now." She removed her hat, placed it on her lap, and tossed her hair, feeling a calmness she hadn't felt in very long time.

"Why did you suggest a hotdog?" she said. "I mean, you've never been to New York. I mean, how did you know?"

"Which one of those would you like me to answer first?"

"I guess I was stammering."

He gave her an affectionate look. "It's okay. I've always heard about the famous hotdog, so I couldn't leave without trying one."

While Jack downed his hotdog, she sat closer to him. She touched the pilot wings sewn above his left breast pocket, feeling the background—soft threads of white silk edged with black, the initials RAF in the center surrounded by a brown laurel wreath.

"What does RAF mean?" she said.

He smiled. "Royal Air Force."

"A flyer."

"Bomber pilot," he said.

"Sounds dangerous."

"Danger is part of war."

"Aren't you an American?" she said.

"An American is restricted from getting into the war, because of the neutrality laws so I pretended to be Canadian."

"Why are you doing this? I mean, I know you said Britain needs help, but America's not in the war."

"Why am I doing it?" he said and she nodded. "Oh I don't know, courage, honor, sacrifice, pick one. It just seemed like a good idea, and it won't be long before we're drawn into the heat of it."

"Why do you say that?"

"War seems inevitable. Isolationist sentiment in America is waning. It's just a matter of time."

Sarah noticed Jack glance again at her uneaten hotdog sitting beside her. "Why don't you let me treat you to dinner this evening?"

"Dinner?"

"Yes."

"I guess that will be alright." Why not? She couldn't remember when she had so much pleasure.

He rose from the park bench and took her hand. "I'll walk you to your hotel. Where are you staying?"

"Across the park at the Le Grand Chateau Hotel." Standing beside him, she turned and pointed to the impressive building extending above the tree tops heavy with green touching the flawless June sky.

"Oh, over there?" His finger followed hers.

"Yes." She laughed at his playful manner. She found herself slipping her arm into his, as they walked along the flowers through Central Park in the late afternoon sun.

"Everything is more beautiful just before dusk, the colors illuminated," she said.

It seemed he didn't hear a word she said, finding it difficult to take his eyes from her. The way her hair twisted in soft curls, her eyes sparkled when she smiled.

"Extraordinary," Jack said.

Chapter 6

"I'll meet you here in the lobby at six o'clock." Jack told Sarah and she agreed. She stepped into the elevator and he gazed at the elevator doors long after they closed if only to hold her image in his mind. Then he turned and walked to the front desk of the Le Grande Chateau Hotel. The clerk, a man in his early thirties, was distributing the daily mail, stuffing it into three by six inch wooden boxes lining the wall behind the desk.

"Hello," Jack said to gain the clerk's attention, and the clerk turned to address the potential guest.

"How can I help you, sir?" the clerk smiled.

"I'm Lieutenant Jack Karsen. Do you have a dining room in your hotel?"

"Yes, we do."

"May I asked, is it very expensive? I can't afford much on an enlisted man's salary."

The clerk looked at Jack's uniform. It was general knowledge that a soldier's pay was thirty-one dollars a month, considerably less than the minimum wage of forty-eight dollars a month.

"Would you wait here one moment, lieutenant?" The clerk disappeared into the backroom then reappeared with an older, equally well dressed gentleman who introduced himself.

"Lieutenant Karsen, I'm the manager at the hotel, and I understand you wish to reserve dinner at the Saint-Veran restaurant here in our hotel."

"Yes sir, but—"

Jack was interrupted by the manager. "Will you be staying with us at the Le Grand Chateau?"

"No, I just arrived this morning," Jack said.

"How long is your stay in New York?" The manager continued his inquiry.

"Two nights."

"We have the penthouse suite available overlooking Central Park. Will that be satisfactory?" Before Jack could reply, the manager added, "We will be most happy to have you be our guest, lieutenant. The accommodation for your stay is entirely complimentary."

Jack was speechless. The cost for a standard room at the Le Grand Chateau Hotel was three times an average room in New York City.

The hotel clerk tapped the manager on the shoulder and pulled him aside, then cupped his hand over his mouth and whispered in the manager's ear: "The penthouse suite has been reserved by the Coffer family."

"They will understand," the manager said in a normal tone of voice, indicating there was no debate.

The manager returned to the front desk. "And the hotel will make a reservation at the Saint-Veran restaurant this evening? Will there be two for dinner?"

"Yes sir, six o'clock."

"A very special person?"

"Yes sir."

"Dinner and dancing for two…six o'clock," the manager said. "We have a very nice table right at the dance floor. It's one of our best and secluded enough for private conversation."

"Gee, that's swell."

"The valet will take you to your suite. Do you have luggage?"

"It's in a locker at the train station," Jack said.

"Leave the key and one of the staff will bring it to your suite."

"That's awfully nice of the hotel. I can't thank you enough. I'm deeply grateful, sir. I don't know how I can thank you."

The manager looked at Jack struggling to find the right words in an attempt to show his depth of appreciation. These were dark days for all of Europe. Going to fight for Britain helped keep America out of the war. If Adolf Hitler who had swallowed up most of Europe, succeeded in conquering the island of Great Britain, the dictator's next doorstep was America.

"It is we, who thank you lieutenant…" the manager said, "…for what you're doing in the war."

Chapter 7

In the lobby of the Le Grand Chateau Hotel, Jack waited for Sarah, pacing the floor, stopping to look toward the elevator every time the doors opened. The hotel clerk standing at the front desk, smiled amusingly, watching Jack thinning the soles of his shoes.

It was difficult for Jack to believe he was a guest at a New York landmark built during the turn of the century. The lobby was a masterful creation of marble finishes, stone columns, elegant patterned mosaic floor, and the bronze and crystal chandelier hanging gracefully from a coffered ceiling was dazzling, radiating sparkling light across the lobby. Such extravagance and beauty. Some people called the hotel the twenty-five story mythical castle with its French Renaissance chateau, architectural style. What a magical place it was for him. Coming from a small town where a youth had never left his roots, New York was beyond his imagination.

And the hotel was treating him like a king. Not only did the manager send up someone to shave him and draw a bath, they sent his uniform to be cleaned and pressed. To top it, the establishment delivered a corsage to his room to give to Sarah. And how could he be so lucky to find Sarah, someone utterly fabulous.

Then, the elevator doors opened, and there she was. A

deep smile came to his face. How could she possibly be more beautiful? Absolutely elegant in a silk V neck dress with a swinging skirt, but of course there was the proper three quarter length sleeves to cover her arms and shoulders. But more, a demure dress she had chosen that would be appropriate for any occasion, even a simple restaurant since she had no idea where the soldier was entertaining her.

When she came close to him her perfume was intoxicating, reminding him of fresh cut flowers brought in from the fields, and her dress—a cloudless sky— made her eyes deeper.

"Hello, Jack."

He stood there, staring, dumbfounded. A canvas could never describe her beauty.

"Is that for me?" she said, referring to the corsage he held in his hand.

"Oh," he laughed, realizing he was daydreaming. "It's for you." He handed her the corsage.

"Gardenias, thank you."

Jack followed her as she walked to the lobby mirror where she removed the corsage wrapped in cellophane and pinned the gardenias to the shoulder of her dress. Standing behind her he saw what the mirror reflected—love.

Then she turned to Jack, reaching for his hand. "So where are you taking me, soldier?"

"I'd like to take you to the moon, but would the Saint-Veran restaurant do?"

She laughed. "Here at the hotel?"

"Oh, is that not alright?""

"Sure, but—"

"Compliments of the hotel. They've been swell. They even gave me the penthouse suite."

"Really? Maybe I should join the RAF."

Chapter 8

"Lieutenant Karsen, we have your table ready." The maître d'' of the Saint-Veran restaurant, grabbed two menus from a shelf in his podium. "Come right this way, please," he requested of Jack and Sarah, extending his hand to point the way.

The restaurant was no less grand and ornate than the lobby of the hotel. Marble columns topped with bronze capitals rose to the thirty foot ceiling, and the walls were of Caen stone. Scores of mirrors lined the western wall, and tables circled around a large dance floor. Most impressive was the stained glass ceiling, inspired by the Floral Garden restaurant in the Bordeaux Chateau Hotel in Paris.

Jack and Sarah settled down at a table at the edge of the dance floor, close to the band's platform. The evening's music was scheduled to begin within the hour.

Jack fingered the edge of the white tablecloth and Sarah smiled. It appeared he was not accustomed to such elegance. Then as Jack viewed the menu, he looked puzzled.

"Can I help you Jack with the menu?" she said.

"I can't quite figure this out. What is Coq Au Vin?"

"Were you looking for more like a hamburger?"

"Actually, that I understand."

Sarah motioned the waiter to their table.

When the waiter appeared, she spoke French, asking him to prepare two hamburgers with sides of "frites". Then she turned back to Jack. "Two hamburgers, soldier, coming up."

"How did you do all that? I mean, I couldn't understand a word you said."

Amused by Jack's reaction, she said, "A restaurant such as this, will prepare anything you want even if it's not on the menu."

Another waiter with a towel draped over his arm, carrying a bottle of Dom Perignon, appeared at Jack's side.

"Will this be acceptable to you, sir?" the waiter said and when Jack looked puzzled again, the waiter said, "Compliments of the management."

Jack smiled, shaking his head. "This trip never ceases to amaze me."

Sarah interceded, "Please tell the management, thank you."

The waiter nodded and proceeded to pour the French Champagne into crystal stemmed glasses, stuffing the bottle with the remaining sparkling wine in a standing bucket of ice close to the table.

Sarah sipped her Champagne, savoring the flavor, then returned her glass to the table. Jack tried his, but appeared recognizably unimpressed.

"So where do you go to meet up with you unit?" she said.

"Canada and to the British Commonwealth facilities where I ship out to Britain."

"You'll be speaking British when you get back," she said, emulating a British accent.

"I'd never be able to do that as well as you," he admired. Then he stared at her in wonderment. He never loved anyone before, never knew what it was, but now he envisioned her by his side, walking among the corn under the hot sun.

"When do you go back to Boston?" he said.

"Tomorrow."

"Stay." He reached for her hand. "I only have a couple days."

She was quiet, appeared thinking. He looked at her and wondered if she would accept his invitation? Had he unintentionally worked his way into her heart as she had his? Will she let the beauty of the day end with a simple goodbye?

"My train leaves in the evening day after tomorrow," he said.

"Where in England will you be stationed?"

"I don't know yet."

"How long will you be gone?"

"If Britain can beat Germany back, maybe a few months, but if America gets into the war, who knows?" He didn't want to talk about the war. Living the war every day would come soon enough.

"What's it like to be an only child?" he said, and she looked amused.

"I don't know. What's it like to have a brother?"

They laughed.

The band had set up on a platform above the dance floor, and Jack's eyes widened when he thought he recognized the band leader walking onto the floor.

"Harry James?" He blurted out.

"Yes." Sarah said.

"My luck keeps getting better all the time. Do you like to dance, Sarah? I'm not good at fancy dancing. Slow is best for me."

"I can manage that."

The band started playing Monaco and Eden's, *You Made Me Love You.* Jack left his chair, walked around the table, took Sarah's hand in his and led her onto the dance floor, pulling her close…so close she could feel his soft breathe against her face.

Chapter 9

"Well, goodnight," Sarah told Jack and inserted the key into the door of her room.

Jack couldn't let her go. He may never see her again. She didn't give him an answer at dinner as to whether she would stay in New York to keep a soldier from being lonely.

"Wait a minute," he said quickly. "I'd like to show you something."

"Alright, what is it?"

"What the hotel is doing for me during my stay. It won't take long. You won't believe it."

Now she was intrigued. She pulled the key away from the lock. They walked back to the elevator, and when they entered, Jack moved closer to the elevator operator. He cupped his hand over his mouth.

"Take us to the penthouse suite." Jack whispered in the elevator operator's ear. As the doors closed, Jack turned to Sarah and said, "Now cover your eyes."

"How mysterious, Jack," she laughed and he helped her place her hands over her eyes.

"Promise you won't peek," he said.

She nodded.

When the elevator doors opened on the twenty-fifth floor, he guided her off the elevator.

"No peeking. Not yet," he instructed as the elevator doors closed and left them alone in the penthouse suite. "Okay, now you can look."

She removed her hands and opened her eyes to a grand, elegant room with a winding staircase, marble fireplace, grand piano and lavishly decorated even to the finest eighteenth century furniture.

"It's a swell place." He took her hand, pulling her into the room.

She smiled, amused. A glorious palace in his eyes, no doubt. Apparently he must have thought she had never seen a suite before. She walked around, pretending to be in awe.

"Take a look out here." He opened French doors leading to a balcony overlooking Central Park. She followed him into the night where lights from the New York's skyline twinkled beyond the park.

"I think you're quite lucky, lieutenant."

"My luck was meeting you," he said, passion in his voice.

"Well, it's been a wonderful evening, Jack. I think I'll go to my room now." She started to walk away.

"No." he said.

When she heard his reply, she stopped and turned, facing him.

"No?" *What's next?* She wondered. *Is this not how it's done? Courtship? Maybe a kiss or two, then the goodnights are said.* It wasn't proper for an unmarried woman to be alone with a man in his room. That much she knew.

He walked to her, placed his hand under her chin, and just before his lips touched hers, he whispered, "No." Then his kisses came soft with passion, long and tender, moving down her neck, his breath hot on her skin. The room seemed to spin...a fire in her she never felt before.

She pulled the comb from her hair, letting the curls fall across her shoulders. What was she doing? What was she thinking? It seemed wrong. Yet, how could it be so wrong when it seemed so natural? The first moment she saw him, she felt it to be true. There was no denying it, she wanted him just as much as it appeared he wanted her, maybe more.

Still holding her close to him as if their bodies were one, he reached around and unzipped the back of her dress. He slid the silk down to reveal her shoulders, still further exposing the soft part of a woman's body. Kissing her there, his lips circling the most tender part, the flames within her raged higher. Amid the passion, their clothes slowly fell away, and for the first time, she saw the nakedness of a man. Not just any man, but this soldier she fell in love with.

He picked her up in his arms and carried her to the bed waiting for the young lovers. Then…more kisses…then what was that sensation…that rapture…the whole room seemed to be filled with love as the universe opened its arms to let her see its magnitude…its glory…as if their love was sealed by celestial forces.

Then as she lay beside him, he pulled her close.

"I want you to hold onto my heart and never let go,"

he said.

"You do, Lieutenant Jack Karsen? Well, I'll keep it safe, I promise." And with that commitment, he closed his eyes and drifted to sleep.

She wondered if he made love to anyone before, but then it didn't matter, for she could tell by the way he touched her, this was different.

Sarah rose from the bed, slipped into one of the guest bath robes, and stepped out onto the balcony. It wasn't quite dawn, the stars still appeared in the sky, the moon full and high.

"Couldn't sleep?" Jack appeared behind her, wrapping his arms around her, drawing his lips close to her ear. "May I join you?" he said softly.

Staring at the sky she welcomed his arms, feeling the warmth of his tenderness. "It's so lovely out here, the moon is so full you can almost touch it."

He came around beside her, and reached for her hand, holding it tight. He looked at the sky and said, "The moon is a miraculous creation, even though it looks cold, barren and lifeless. If the moon didn't exist or wasn't precisely the size it is, or even move at the speed in which it spins, or off a fraction of a degree in its distance from the sun, there would be no life on earth. Appears too obvious that there has to be a creator to all this."

What else don't I know about you Jack Karsen? She thought. *You already have my heart, now you want to be sure to keep it.*

"See that star…" he pointed to the brightest star among the stars in the heavens, "…that's Polaris often called the North Star," he said, and she looked to where he indicated. "It sits directly above Earth's North Pole. True north lies directly under that star. Navigators have used it for centuries to keep them from losing their way. No matter where you are on earth, it's always right there." He took her index finger and raising it up toward the heavens, pointed to the North Star. "Wherever I am, wherever I go in this war, just look up there, and you'll see me."

Chapter 10

In the morning Sarah was gone. She had slipped out of the penthouse early with no mention that she was leaving. Jack called her room with no answer. He dressed and took the elevator to the lobby. The ride seemed forever.

"Miss Wescott is not in her room." Jack told the clerk at the hotel's front desk.

"She checked out this morning," the clerk said.

At first, Jack thought he had said or done something wrong, or perhaps he presumed too much. But as he thought back, it didn't appear to him that was the case. It was so right as if it was meant to be.

"Nice young lady. She's a Wescott, you know," the desk clerk said matter-of-factly. "Stays with us once a year, always comes with her mother. First time she came alone."

"Wescott?" Jack said.

"Yes, upper-crust of Boston society." the clerk added.

Jack dismissed what the clerk had said for what did that have to do with two people in love. Then thoughts loaded his mind. *How will I find her? Tell her what happened last night was honest and real.*

"Did she say where she was going?" Jack said.

"Boston. She must have been in a hurry. She booked a commercial flight, canceling her train reservation."

As the clerk turned away to retrieve a note, Jack started to walk away. When the clerk turned back to Jack, the clerk called to him.

"Lieutenant Karsen?"

Jack approached the clerk again.

"Miss Wescott asked me to tell you she would see you off at your train tomorrow evening."

Chapter 11

At the Wescott mansion, the butler, Harrington, met Sarah at the entry. She handed him her gloves and handbag. The Wescott chauffer who had followed her inside, set her suitcase on the floor and left. The butler closed the entry door then turned to Sarah.

"Your father and mother are in the library."

Walking across the marble floor of the central hall toward the library, she passed the grand staircase with its intricate wrought iron railing winding up to a second and third floor. In the ceiling above the stairwell was a stained glass skylight depicting a Revolutionary War scene of the first shot fired at Lexington just after dawn.

Home to the Wescotts for generations, the Georgian style mansion was built in 1750 and stood among other prestigious mansions on Beacon Street. Overlooking Boston Common the nation's oldest park, the mansion was once occupied by the British during the Siege of Boston after the Battle at Lexington in 1775. Some of the rooms were used to house the British wounded.

The mansion's forty room interior was an elegant reproduction of a European palace, and furnished with the finest furniture designed and crafted by Europe's best craftsmen. Portraits of the Wescott family members from the time of the founding fathers hung in each of the first floor rooms. Among the mansion's guests were George Washington and Beacon Hill neighbor, John Hancock, first governor of Massachusetts and the first signer of the Declaration of Independence. The third floor had a sweeping view of the famous Boston Harbor where one could have seen British ships arriving to occupy Boston in October, 1768. All part of her family's long history she had been brought up to appreciate and respect.

Reaching the library, Sarah placed her hand on the door's latch handle, holding it tight, hesitating before opening it. What lay beyond the door, inevitably, would determine her fate.

Early that morning after she had left Jack, she phoned her father from Le Grand Chateau Hotel.

"I met a soldier, father," she said, excitement in her voice. "He's wonderful. A bomber pilot. I'd like you to meet him, but he's leaving for the war. His train leaves tomorrow evening, and—"

"You are to come home immediately," Winston Wescott had said and abruptly hung up. This did not appear hopeful. But what did she expect? She apparently took him by surprise, caught up in the magical moments with Jack, forgetting everything else. Love will blind reality.

She had taken a plane instead of the train to return home so she would have enough time to fly back to New York to see Jack at the train station before he left for the war.

There could be no further delay. Taking a deep breath

she entered the library, slowly closing the door behind her.

At the other end of the library, Winston and Charlotte Wescott waited. They appeared as if swallowed up by the depth and magnitude of the cavernous room, reminiscent of a mid12th century Gothic cathedral in Europe. The stone walls soared vertically to reach a Caen stone vaulted ceiling with pointed arches that swept upward with height and grace across the entire room.

A mahogany bookshelf holding leather bound, priceless first editions lined an entire wall. It wrapped around a six foot fireplace where a man could stand in without touching his head. Cathedral windows graced the opposite wall where Prism light streamed through beveled glass, bestowing a heavenly appearance across the library.

At the far end of the library, a colossal stain glass window spilled its multi-colored light across her father's executive desk. Elegance and beauty befitting a family of extraordinary wealth. As a child, the library reminded Sarah of a church with missing pews. She never knew what her father had in mind when he redesigned and expanded the library of the Wescott mansion years ago. Perhaps Winston Wescott was trying to reach heaven and this way, he wouldn't be far from it.

The room seemed cold, unlike Sarah had ever known, and she felt a chill which confirmed her assumption that there would be strong words exchanged.

Sarah walked down the scarlet carpet, a runner the

length of the room, which lay over a shiny oak floor. Each of her steps seemed heavier than the last as if the guillotine awaited her and fear bordered on sheer terror.

Winston Wescott stood behind the desk in front of the stained glass window. Near six foot he was a robust man, partly owed to genetics and in part to a healthy appetite for rich foods. He had thick white hair, attractive to women, and envied by most men his age.

Charlotte sat demurely on a settee near the desk, her hands folded in her lap. A soft spoken, slender and petite woman of quiet grace, she had a patience her husband lacked. Her dark hair was touched with streaks of silver.

When Sarah neared, Winston had a disappointed look on his face, his hand on his hip. He pulled a watch hanging on a long chain from the vest pocket of his suit. Drawing it up, he looked at the time then stuffed it back in its hiding place.

"Father…mother." Sarah greeted quietly, breaking the silence, apprehension in her voice.

Charlotte rose from the settee and with great anticipation, she went to greet her daughter.

"Sarah, darling," she said softly, "your father and I have been waiting for you since your phone call this morning." She took Sarah's hand and kissed her on the check. "Why you're trembling dear?"

"I'm alright, mother."

"I'll have Harington bring in some hot tea."

"No, thank you."

"Come here and sit down next to me," Charlotte

coaxed. "Did you find the weather pleasant in New York? It is lovely in June." Charlotte pointed out as they walked to the settee and sat down.

"I did." But Sarah failed to tell her about the handkerchief given to the soldier.

During the conversation between Sarah and Charlotte, Winston tapped his foot on the carpet in short continuous thumps as if he was keeping beat to a drum. The sound was soft, but acutely evident. Sarah watched her father through the corner of her eye. He had yet to speak, and it was his thunder she worried about. She didn't want to upset him or her mother for that matter. Meeting Jack just happened through no fault of her own.

"Your father told me you met a soldier?" Charlotte inquired, gently, visibly attempting to get to the bottom of what she and Winston apparently viewed as a serious issue.

"How old is this soldier, dear?"

"Twenty-two."

"How did you happen to meet him?"

"Charlotte!" Winston slammed his fist on the desk, his deep watchful eyes widened as he shouted. Charlotte and Sarah looked up simultaneously, startled. Winston had enough of this garden party prattle and had no interest in the niceties of the day. He had been pacing the floor for at least an hour before Sarah's arrival. Family matters, in his judgment, were to run smoothly as did his business.

"This is not afternoon tea with nonsensical chit chat!" he told Charlotte.

It seemed Charlotte was slightly embarrassed by her husband's attitude toward her, but appeared to dismiss it as she usually did. Circumstances required a heavy hand. After all, his was the final word.

With no delay, Winston turned his attention to Sarah.

"Your phone call to me was quite disturbing," Winston said. "You need to explain to your mother and me what is going on here, Sarah?"

"I just want to wait before I get married."

"Wait?" Winston was unable to believe what he just heard.

"Yes."

Winston glared at her. "Wait for this soldier? Did he have the audacity to ask you to wait for him?"

Sarah lowered her eyes which indicated to him the answer.

"I thought so."

"Father, you don't understand, I love him."

"That's utterly ridiculous. You've known this soldier for one day."

"I can't explain it, father. I can't even explain it to myself. It's just something you feel that's right…and well…father, I'm not sure I should marry George Minton…I mean, I'm not sure I want to."

"Sarah, you don't mean that." Charlotte looked surprised at her daughter's confession. She appeared as if she could no longer stay silent. She seemed to be contemplating the long term effects of such a decision.

"It's been all arranged." Charlotte pointed out. "Once

you completed finishing school to learn the social graces and etiquette necessary to further your husband's position in Boston society, you would marry. The invitations have gone out."

"I know how important this is to you mother—"

Winston threw up his hands. "Charlotte, please! I'll handle this!" This appeared far more serious than Winston had anticipated.

"What's this all about Sarah? What is this foolishness you have your head wrapped around?" he said.

Sarah didn't answer.

"Winston, calm yourself," Charlotte said. "After all, Sarah is not one of your employees not living up to your expected level of competency. Sarah is only a girl of twenty. You should consider handling this matter more gently."

"Charlotte! Our daughter goes off and meets some stranger, and you want me to address this calmly?"

"You're right, Winston, we should have never let her go to New York alone."

Winston redirected his attention back to Sarah.

"Where does this soldier come from? What do we know about him? What's his background?" He fired rapid questions, his assertive authority changed little, and his voice grew restless.

"He's from Iowa."

"Iowa!" Surprise in Winston's voice.

"It's beautiful when he speaks of it."

Frustrated, Winston threw up his hands again. "Cow

country! Farmer! Dirt on his clothes! He has nothing to give you. Furthermore, he goes into the war with nothing, and he'll come out of the war with nothing. He may never come home, and if he does, he may come home as half a man. And what are his employment opportunities? A mechanic, a soda jerk in a drug store?"

"Could you give him a job when he gets home?" she asked timidly and Winston just shook his head, rubbing his forehead in exasperation. Every word from Sarah's mouth made Winston angrier. Furthermore, it was difficult for him to believe that she was his own seed. But then, perhaps he owed her behavior to youth and the lack of wisdom.

"Sarah," Winston said firmly, "you have no idea what's involved here. There's no future with this soldier. You can't shake the dirt off a farmer's shoes."

Her heart began to race. It appeared that Sarah was not winning against Winston's strength.

"Do you understand, we are not the same people as this farmer." Winston asserted. "We don't think the same way. The Wescott legacy should be foremost in your mind and your marriage to George Minton who has the same background."

In Winston's judgment there was no better choice than George. He was considered old Boston—well revered family that claimed its roots from America's founders. More importantly, George was the son of a shipbuilding tycoon with a vast amount of wealth—old money handed down for generations, mostly accumulated through intermarriage. Combining George's wealth with the Wescotts' multi-million dollar investment company, vastly appealed to Winston's head for finance if not his greed. A perfect merger of two family fortunes where one would not want for anything. Winston was selling his own daughter off as an investment. All things were for advantage. And at age twenty-six, George was not too old, yet not too young and he was a Harvard man like Winston. Smart men appealed to Winston.

In all good conscience, Winston would not tolerate a marriage into new money—money that was acquired by a man's own right and the sweat of his brow in the present generation. Marrying some lowly soldier of no means whatsoever was unacceptable and furthermore, not tolerated. Marriage is about tradition and duty. The heart has little or no consideration.

Winston looked around the room, reminding himself of how wealth is accumulated. He was devoid of humanity beyond the existence of riches which he had inherited, and worked hard to cultivate into extreme wealth. He had a gift of knowing when to buy and sell on the market, investment strategy learned from his father, Philip, and his father before him, down through the generations. Philip made the bulk of the estate in the bull market of 1916. Then Winston, sensing trouble ahead, liquidated his stocks right before the 1929 Crash, and increased the Wescott wealth fourfold.

It would not be thrown away by some frivolous idea, daughter or not, who had all the benefits without the knowledge of the dynamics behind it. He could not nor would he allow mistakes and this he considered to be a catastrophic one, which prompted him to ask Sarah the question:

"You didn't encourage this soldier, did you?"

"No." Sarah said.

"Has he spoken of marriage?"

"No."

"And he won't. He's just a soldier on leave, looking for a good time, taking advantage of a young girl."

"Winston!" Charlotte gasped, raising her eyebrows. It wasn't social correctness to speak of such morals, even between a family member. Winston should know Sarah would never dishonor the Wescott family.

Winston ignored Charlotte, desiring to bring the matter to a conclusion. He stared at Sarah, waiting for her to admit or deny intimacy.

"It wasn't like that, father. You understand, he's leaving tomorrow, I may never see him again."

"Precisely." Winston punctuated the word.

"I'm a grown woman now. I should be able to make my own decisions."

"A grown woman should be wise enough to know her place in the world." Winston told Sarah. "The idea that you would even consider tarnishing this family's good name, thinking of something so irresponsible is sinful."

"Mother?" Sarah pleaded, her last hope of defense.

Sitting next to Sarah, Charlotte took Sarah's hand in hers. "You are to be married in two weeks. You're pledged to George on your father's word. Your father could never embarrass George's father and old friend Bradford Minton, or live through such embarrassment himself."

Sarah's eyes welled up with tears. She would get no help from her mother. It was evident Charlotte had accepted her own fate, now it was expected of her daughter to follow suit to speak well, know the arts, and as a Boston socialite to be a philanthropist.

"You are so young," Charlotte said. "What do you know about love? You're just a child. You must let us make the decisions for you. George is solid." It appeared Charlotte spoke from experience as if someone in her past had said those same words.

Winston walked around to the front of the desk, sat on its edge, and stared Sarah straight in the eye. There was a moral force within him that would not bend. He was prepared to solve this problematic issue and quick.

"Now you will listen to me, Sarah," he said firmly. "We will hear no more of this nonsense. Your position in Boston society commands a certain responsibility. You will marry George Minton as planned, and get on with your life as you know it. I forbid you to see this soldier again, and furthermore you will forget him.

"We will speak no more of this inside or outside the family. The event will remain untainted by scandal. Is that understood?"

Charlotte and Sarah said nothing, but appeared to know his demand was made clear.

"In the morning, it will all be forgotten," he said, confirming it, if not in his own mind, in theirs. "Years from now, you'll thank me for saving you from an ill fate."

Chapter 12

Among the many faces on the railway platform, Jack searched for Sarah's, nervously shuffling back and forth like an expectant father. His spirit was high. Waiting for this moment, anticipating her arrival, almost overcame him, thinking nothing but of her the last two days.

Time was passing. The train was leaving any moment. Where was she? Why wasn't she coming? He was afraid he would go through life without her, touch her soft skin, sink deep into those blue eyes. He feared that more than what lay ahead for him—dark days of the war.

Then he heard a voice in the distance he thought, calling his name. As the voice came nearer…yes… it was his name.

"Calling Mr. Karsen."

"Over here!" Jack called back. The crowd on the railway platform opened up to reveal the voice. A boy about sixteen years old, wearing a Western Union uniform, moved with purpose, appearing to take his job most seriously.

Approaching Jack, the boy said, "Mr. Jack Karsen?"

"Yes."

"Telegram, soldier," he said after he noticed Jack's uniform. This did not appear good. A feeling of despair fell over Jack.

The boy handed Jack a tablet he pulled out of his pocket, requiring Jack's signature. Then the boy stuffed an envelope in Jack's fist.

Jack began to offer a tip, and the boy said, "That's okay. Good luck, soldier."

Jack thanked him, and the boy left as quickly as he came, disappearing among the passengers and well-wishers still standing on the railway platform.

Tearing the seal, he opened the telegram…

> Jack,
>
> I can never see you again. Please don't ask why. Know that you take a part of me with you.
>
> Sarah.

…No war injury he may sustain would be worse than the wound of her words. Jack stood motionless on the railway platform, staring at nothing, his hand still clinging to the telegram. Was it a brief acquaintance? It couldn't be. Her heart spoke to him.

He looked toward the station's main entrance to the railway platform, still hoping her image would appear that she had second thoughts after sending the telegram.

The train whistle blew. Then the conductor called several times, "All aboard!" as he walked among those yet remaining on the railway platform, until he reached the last car and Jack standing alone. He saw the sad look on Jack's face. Someone important no doubt the soldier needed to see.

The train began moving slowly from the station.

"If you're leaving, soldier, you'll have to climb aboard," the conductor informed him, breaking into Jack's faraway thoughts.

Jack crumpled the telegram deep in his fist then tossed it away. He hopped onto the last car of the train, followed by the conductor who walked around Jack, then entered the car.

As the train moved away from the station, Jack stood on the platform of the last car, watching the station fade into the distance and with it, the most incredible day of his life. She walked out of his life as quickly as she came in, and he would never be the same. Forever in his mind. Forever in his heart. All the tomorrows.

He should have told her that he loved her, but she must have known. A man doesn't give himself to a woman the way he did without giving of himself completely.

As he watched the station slowly diminish from sight, and felt the wind, stirred by the moving train, blow across his face, the loss dug deep within him. He never felt so alone.

I should have told her that I love her… he whispered into the wind…*I'll tell her when the war is over. I'll tell her then…I'll tell her then.*

Chapter 13

"You must let men have their way." Charlotte told her daughter on what Sarah was to expect on her wedding night.

As Charlotte sat next to Sarah on the settee in Sarah's bedroom on the second floor of the Wescott mansion, Charlotte nervously adjusted the pillow behind her back, fidgeting mostly. Such a discourse was not something Charlotte appeared to be comfortable with, but it was her duty as a mother to educate her daughter. Use of the proper choice of words was imperative for such a delicate subject not normally spoken of.

"It is not meant to be pleasurable to you, but to them and for you to produce heirs." Charlotte spoke quietly, reverently as if they were attending a wake.

"Women should have no desires of their own, but only to please their husband's needs. Follow what is natural to him," Charlotte added.

What did her mother mean—his pleasure? Should Sarah not witness pleasure too? Or was she to hide her pleasure as women were expected to hide their intellect. But Sarah dare not ask.

"Being married to George won't be easy." Charlotte moved closer to Sarah on the settee, and now spoke in almost a whisper.

"Easy?" Sarah said. "Why?"

"A Minton or a Wescott man is pretty much cut from the same mold. Their uncompromising position in life is so consuming that their thoughts are seldom from it. We women are just there as part of the package. The important thing is to have children to carry on the family name. That's what it's truly all about.

"Don't think too harshly of your father." Charlotte advised Sarah. "He means well. Bad feelings should be set aside. He just doesn't want you to put your life on hold for something so uncertain."

"Did you love father when you married him?"

"He possessed my heart."

"Do you know what that means, mother?"

"It was the right thing to do."

"But did you love each other?" Sarah pressed for an answer.

"You mean like you talk about your soldier?"

"Yes," Sarah said, but her mother would give her no answer, and a distant look came to Charlotte's eyes as if she wanted to say something she held in heart that no one knew.

"What shall I do, mother?"

"You must force yourself to forget him. Focus on practicality, your position in life and George."

Chapter 14

The wedding ceremony materialized as planned. Elected officials and all of Boston's elite, old money and new, attended the Wescott-Minton wedding in what was considered the affair of the year. It was the day Winston had longed for. Increasing the Wescott wealth was paramount in his plan, and he seemed to dwell on the extreme satisfaction no one could understand, except a man who lusts for power, money can command.

Chatter and laughter of wedding guests swept over the Wescott garden where the nuptials would take place. The sweet notes of a string quartet playing Vivaldi's *Largo from Winter* found their way past the open French doors and into the second floor sitting-room of the Wescott mansion where Sarah prepared for the eventful day.

Yards and yards of ivory European silk billowed around her, flowing to a six foot train. The high neck, bodice and long sleeves of lace were clusters with sequins and pearls. Fresh flowers crowned her hair where auburn ringlets pulled back at the sides, dropped gently onto tiny satin buttons enclosing the back of the dress. A veil edged with lace appliques fell to the length of the train. Even her satin shoes were embellished with sequins and pearls.

Gardenias, a reminder of Jack, were among the white

roses, stephanotis and calla lilies in a bouquet cascading to touch the floor length hem. A twelve carat, round cut diamond hung from her neck by a delicate platinum chain. No expense was spared to create such elegance.

She moved closer to the pier mirror reflecting her image, examining how pale she looked. She pinched her cheeks to draw color into them, but there was not much she could do about the dark circles appearing under her eyes. She hardly slept a wink the night before. Not from the usual nervousness and excitement a bride experiences the night before her wedding, but because she worried about spending a lifetime with George when her heart belonged to another. She touched the bouquet to her nose and the velvet softness of the gardenias to relive the memory the sweet scent brought her.

Louise Wescott, Sarah's grandmother, entered the room, gliding gracefully in a full length dark blue dress, her thick white hair coiffured in a special style for the occasion of tight curls about her round face. She was smiling, beaming with pride, a twinkle in her gray blue eyes. She had just come from the public rooms on the first floor, greeting friends and old acquaintances. She walked directly to Sarah standing in front of the pier mirror. Never before had she seen such an elaborate dress.

"Hello, my darling girl. You are so beautiful that you take my breath away. Your mother told me about the dress, but I had no idea how royal it is."

"Yes, beautiful," Sarah said with no emotion.

"Why so sad? What is it, child?"

When Sarah didn't respond, Louise Wescott nodded and said, "You've fallen in love, or that's what you think it is."

Sarah looked surprised.

"Oh, your father told me all about it. You're quite taken with this soldier. I know there's to be no talk about it, but I must help put things to a close." Louise handed Sarah her handkerchief when tears came to Sarah's eyes.

"Oh my dear, something happens like that to every young girl. They have a brief flirtation and think its forever. In my day, a lot of young men fancied me, but I kept my wits about me and you're expected to do the same."

"But this is different," Sarah said.

Louise patted her on the shoulder. "There, there now, dry those tears. You think you've lost the love of your life. No love is ever lost, my dear. He will always be in your heart where your memories live. Now you must let it go. No good will come to you hanging on. You're use to a different life than this soldier can provide for you. You would wake up one day and ask yourself why did you do that? Doesn't have any earmarks of lasting. Our kind marries for position and money. It's the sensible thing." Louise seemed to strongly believe.

Louise was a woman of great elegance, and her beauty although faded, still radiated in her wisdom. She held little of Winston's fiery disposition. Sarah could only imagine that Winston possessed more of his own father's traits, but it would be difficult for Sarah to judge. Her grandfather died before she was born. Her grandmother had always been on her side in the past, but this time Louise appeared to agree with Charlotte.

"Your inner spirit survives on how your past has conditioned you," Louise said. "Your future is with George. The family adores him." She followed her sermon with a kiss on Sarah's cheek.

"Now don't you shed another tear, you'll ruin your makeup, and stain that white dress. Powder your nose and get on with your life. Today is the happiest day of your life. Hold your head high. Remember, you're a Wescott, descendant of the earliest English Colonists—Blue Blood of Boston."

Sarah watched Louise leave with the same determined step as when she arrived, appearing satisfied that the mere sound of her voice was the cure for everything. Sarah realized she was alone in this. No one understood. All they did, they did for the greater good—their good.

With the veil pulled over her face and the dress so voluminous she looked like she was lost in a cloud, Sarah came down the stairs of the central hall. Garlands of gardenias laced the banister winding down three flights of the grand staircase. Flowers were everywhere stationed in the garden and the formal rooms of the first floor. Their smell of sweetness spilled from tall urns, sweeping the full scent of summer through the wedding festivities.

Sarah walked through the drawing room to her father waiting at the French doors leading to the garden. Stuffed in the traditional morning suit of a single button tailcoat, matching grey trousers and vest, white silk shirt and tie, Winston beamed with noticeable pride. A single white rose in his lapel, distinguished him as a member of the wedding party apart from the other guests dressed in tailcoats.

At least the women had a choice, except they were required to wear floor length dresses, unembellished, muted colors—-no red or black, and would be denied admittance if dressed to the contrary. They were required to send a photo of the dress and attach a sample of the material for approval, including George's mother, although the mother of the bride and groom were allowed a simple embellishment to set them apart.

As the time of the nuptials drew near, guests were encouraged to take their seats staged on each side of the processional path where wild roses spilled from urns sitting on tall pedestals along the aisle. Winston had a fetish for promptness, so there was a need for guests to be seated before the grandfather clock in the central hall, struck five. The Press was allowed only a few photos of Boston society's event of the year for as a Boston Brahmin, the Wescott family restricted newspaper coverage. Only a private wedding photographer was allowed further admittance.

Trumpets sounded and the string quartet began to play Wagner's *Bridal Chorus*, signaling the beginning of the wedding procession. Winston took Sarah's arm and tucked it into his. He smiled in satisfaction and nodded.

Not even a princess of noble blood could have been dressed finer. And the gods could not have given them a more beautiful day. For the last week in June, the weather was a pleasant seventy-five degrees.

"You look lovely, my dear," Winston said still smiling. Sarah returned the smile, but it was empty. Winston saw something missing in her eyes only he, as a father, would see—a lack of sparkle a bride should have on her wedding day. If it was that soldier, in the course of time he would fade even beyond memory, Winston seemed sure of it.

Walking the white runner strewn with pink rose petals, the sequins on the bodice of her dress sparkled beneath her veil in the late afternoon sun that cast a glow across the garden. As Sarah passed, the guests smiled widely. One moment in time when neither man nor woman would have a care or worry enter their mind.

Through her veil, Sarah could see George waiting at the end of the processional path under the flower covered arbor Winston had built especially for the occasion. George was near six foot, ordinary in his appearance, brown hair, and eyes. He was not strikingly handsome as Jack who could quickly turn an eye and not at all full of life where the world held immeasurable things to discover. Rather George was quiet, reserved to the point of boredom.

George stood solemn, stuffed in his morning suit, no expression on his face, his hands folded in front of him. He appeared calm, none of the normal jitters a groom would have. She could hear her mother's words over and over again: *George is solid.*

Sarah took her place next to George in front of the minister. Winston retired to the front row next to Charlotte who chose a simple pink floor length dress, embellished at the beltline for mother of the bride. Sitting next to Charlotte, Louise smiled, appearing evermore confident that nothing now would interfere with the Wescotts' treasured status.

George's father and mother sat directly across the aisle from Winston and Charlotte. Both were grinning from ear to ear. It was a special day for Bradford and Ellen Minton, their only child married. Winston was an only child and Charlotte's one sibling died of the fever at age fourteen. Bradford and Ellen Minton appeared an uncommon couple. Both were short and plump. Ellen had a full head of white hair, and Bradford was nearly bald. Who would have thought they were George's parents? Only resemblance—George inherited Ellen's eye color. Ellen sat so close to Bradford, it was difficult to tell who was wearing the dark rose, floor length dress with a small bit of lace at the neckline.

Ellen Minton was a quiet woman, and unlike Charlotte who would sometimes disagree with Winston, Ellen always agreed on all matters rather than voice an opinion. She adored George, smothering him with attention, appearing to the point of suffocation. The Mintons were all the same—cold, proper, respectable. George was all they aspired him to be, forming his life like melting steel.

Being an only child was all Sarah and George had in common, besides being born Boston Upper-Crust.

The preacher's voice droned on. Sarah didn't hear a word of the introduction. All she could think of was Jack, the telegram and never seeing him again. And when she said her vows, pledging commitment to George…"to honor, and obey, until death do us part"…it was to Jack she imagined saying those words. Why couldn't she stop thinking of Jack? Her life had been planned for her. As her grandmother had said, "Your future is with George."

George slipped a band heavy with a single row of diamonds on her finger. She would wear it daily, except for social occasions. Then she would replace it with the ten carat emerald cut diamond, Jack saw on her finger.

After the preacher pronounced them man and wife, George smiled pleasingly. Then he took her hands, one after the other and pressed them to his lips as if it were their first introduction. Apparently it wasn't deemed appropriate in his reasoning to show a higher regard in public.

The string quartet played Mendelssohn's rather joyous *Wedding March*, indicating the reception was in full swing. Almost immediately laughter and jubilant voices emulated throughout the garden and the first floor of the mansion.

In every room champagne flowed from fountains and dainty silver cups circled around large crystal bowls where blood orange slices floated in cool wine. A bar in the garden offered heavy drinks for those who required more substantial spirits. Waiters with silver trays, bustled through the rooms, offering guests a variety of finger foods—vodka soaked watermelon cubes, oysters, delicate garlic sausages with rosemary, imported Sicilian cheese, dates bursting with toasted walnut and fresh mint, small silver cups of caviar, tiny marinated lamb riblets with pesto spread, and small crustless sandwiches stuffed with filet mignon, smoke salmon or roasted chicken.

The cake was the whispered envy of the whole affair. A six tier white pound cake with rum custard filling, and whipped cream topping rested on a low pedestal amid pink rose petals scattered randomly across the table. A generous cluster of pink and ivory roses clung to one side of the lower tier of the cake. More circled around climbing to the top to another cluster of roses. Winston had a special light installed to accentuate the masterpiece.

No one in Boston held a social event like Winston and since this was the wedding day of his only offspring, everything had to be flawless. And indeed it was. He had proven himself once again to be the perfect host, providing an array of food and entertainment with all the social graces, befitting a man of his dignity, unmatched by Boston's elite. And now the Wescott-Minton pact was sealed. He couldn't have been more elated.

"I'm delighted they're married." Bradford told Winston as he admirably viewed the gaiety of the moment surrounding them.

"A Wescott event is always considered a stunning event," Winston said.

"Remarkable is the word." A compliment Bradford

gave gladly and one Winston was accustomed to.

"Come with me, Bradford, where we can talk." Winston coaxed, clasping Bradford's shoulder, his six foot frame towering over Bradford's height at five foot, one. "It will only take a few minutes. The guests won't miss us for a short time."

The two men left the garden, and took the elevator to the sitting-room of the second floor family apartment and to another equally ornate part of the mansion. Eighteenth century European furniture covered with fabrics of silk and wool, rested on finely woven area rugs that lay over the mansion's oak floors. Heavy velvet draped across large windows, tied to hooks with cords of golden thread. Ordinarily the library would have been Winston's preferred room, but all of the public rooms on the first floor were filled with wedding guests.

Bradford planted himself at the end of one of the several sofas in the palatial room while Winston sat on the sofa's arm at the far end. Winston reached over and lifted a box of cigars from a long table stretching across the back of the sofa. He offered one to Bradford, but Bradford declined.

"You know I don't smoke, Winston."

"Having the enjoyment of a cigar once in a while is not smoking," Winston said. "Besides I thought the occasion might permit one."

"Hmmm." Bradford gave Winston a sharp look. He agreed with most things Winston's strong personality demanded, but when it came to vices however moderate, that's where he drew the line. Winston knew this.

"Well, whatever." Winston grabbed a cigar from the box and set the box back on the table. He drew the cigar across his nose to smell its sweetness. Then Winston appearing anxious came right to the point.

"Bradford, I don't mean to bring up something quite sensitive, but you did have a conversation with George about how he is to act as a husband?"

"Husband?" Bradford wasn't quite sure what Winston meant.

"How he is to prepare for this evening." Winston lit his cigar, inhaling several long puffs before letting the smoke drift from his mouth in a long stream.

"Prepare?" Bradford still couldn't figure out what Winston was referring to.

"Perform," Winston attempted to clarify.

Bradford thought for a second. "Oh yes," he nodded, finally getting the point. "Everything will go well."

"Excellent."

Bradford smiled.

"And Charlotte, spoke with Sarah last evening," Winston said.

Bradford nodded as if all set.

"I've decided their first born should be named Philip after my father, that's of course if the offspring is a boy." In a fashion of pride, Winston grabbed hold of each side of his coat lapels holding them tight, his cigar clenched between his teeth. "If you have no objections, the second child should take a name from the Minton family."

"It's quite alright with me, Winston," Bradford said, not willing to debate Winston's decision. No one wins against Winston, silver tongue among businessmen and politicians. Bradford was aware that Winston had been offered to run for an elected office, but Winston had explained to Bradford that he thought politics was corrupt, run by a bunch of greedy old men, that most couldn't make their mark in the world with a higher use of their intellect. Winston viewed politicians as puppets who are easily manipulated by the color green. He preferred politics on the sidelines, getting what he wanted by money.

Bradford didn't even find fault with Winston when Winston had told him Sarah and George were going to live with Winston and Charlotte, that Winston had remodeled the third floor of the Wescott mansion, turning it into an apartment for them. Bradford had wanted Sarah and George to take up residence in the Minton mansion, but Winston's excuse to Bradford was: "a girl needs to be close to her mother, you know how that is Bradford."

Bradford knew Winston didn't care if Bradford disagreed. Bradford owed Winston much more than accommodating him in regards to their children's living accommodations. Winston's knowledge of investments helped Bradford build his wealth to greater heights. However unscrupulous Winston may be, Bradford, much like his son, was drawn to people with strength of will.

"Do you think George and Sarah will be in agreement

with the names?" Bradford said.

"There's no question." Winston stated affirmatively.

Bradford nodded apprehensively. Knowing Winston, George and Sarah would be happy even if Winston had to will it into being.

Winston rose from where he sat on the arm of the sofa, walked over to Bradford, and smiled pleasingly, shaking his hand. "Well then, you will at least allow yourself to have a drink. This special day does command it," he added sarcastically, evidently not willing to let Bradford's declined offer of a cigar lay to rest.

Although drinking spirits was a vice in Bradford's opinion, Winston was obviously aware that Bradford had no qualms with washing down one or two every evening. "Medicinal purposes. Stimulates the heart." Bradford was convinced, and undoubtedly didn't care if it appeared hypocritical.

Heading across the room to a table holding glasses and decanters filled with intoxicants, Winston reached for the scotch and poured a generous amount into crystal lowball glasses. Bradford preferred tonic so he added just a touch. Winston walked back to the sofa and planted the scotch in Bradford's hand.

With family matters concluded, the two men downed their drinks and rejoined the celebration. The quiet they just left transformed to laughter and the music from the string quartet that had moved inside from the garden.

When George saw his father and Winston reappear, he pulled Winston aside and drew his attention to Sarah.

From across the drawing room, Sarah was looking at the two of them, a distant, forced look of happiness on her face.

"Sarah looks tired," George said.

"She's just nervous. All the excitement," Winston assured him, ignoring the fact that there may be something deeper. "It's been quite hectic the last week with all the activity here. So many people running about setting everything into play for the ceremony."

"I'm sure you're right, Winston."

"Time to call me father, my boy."

Chapter 15

At seven o'clock with one hour left for the wedding guests to linger, enjoy the surroundings, eat of the sumptuous delights and drink to their gastronomic desire, the wedding couple bid their goodnight. They retired to their apartment on the third floor. Three hours was plenty to make merry. The invitations explicitly stated the ceremony at five, reception following until eight. Winston had no qualms about specifics. After all, no one needs more than three hours for an event and that may even prove too long.

The spacious rooms on the third floor had been fully renovated and newly decorated with deep fall colors and the furniture covered with the finest European fabrics. Cost once again was never a concern for Winston. He may have been selfish with his attention, but generous with material things which he thought made up for his lack of outward affection.

Like Winston and Charlotte's apartment on the second floor, George and Sarah had separate bedrooms with sitting-rooms that adjoined a larger more spacious family room. Procreation was primary, not intimacy.

In Sarah's bedroom, the maid finished helping Sarah remove her wedding gown and slip into a sheer nightgown slit open in the front and tied with a ribbon at the neck.

When a knock was heard on the door between the bedroom and the adjoining sitting-room, the maid looked at Sarah.

"Should I not brush your hair before bed, madam?"

"No time for that. Thank you." Sarah told her and the maid hurriedly retrieved articles of clothing lying on the floor, draping them over a chair. She then left through a hall entrance.

The knock came again, then the door opened slowly, and George poked his head inside, like a child sneaking into a room he was forbidden to enter.

"Are you ready, my dear?"

"Come in George."

With a robe wrapped tight around his body, George entered slowly, closing the door behind him. He walked past Sarah, went to the bed and removed his robe revealing only his undershorts. He pulled the covers away from the bed and slipped in between the sheets.

"I'm ready," he said, tucking the covers tight around his neck.

Why was he behaving that way? Is this what she had to look forward to? She sighed.

She went to the other side of the bed, and turned off the table lamp. Slipping off her nightgown, she slid her nakedness into the bed and under the covers beside him. His head turned to look at her while still holding the covers tight about his neck.

There were no soft kisses, no spoken words of love. It

was over as quick as it began. It appeared as if it was difficult. She wasn't even sure it was pleasurable for him. If she didn't feel somewhat sorry for George, it would almost appear humorous. Then, perhaps George was just nervous. It was apparent he had not been intimate before.

Her mother had described the night as being unnatural to a woman, meant only for a man's pleasure and for a woman to merely procreate, to give into his baser instincts. But Sarah knew what happened behind closed doors, and it was not how her mother spoke of it. It was one of true passion and nothing was more natural than displaying affection when you love someone deeply.

Sarah probably would not have known any different than her quick consummation with George if she hadn't met Jack. She had respectfully listened to her mother as if she knew nothing about things unsaid when all along the night her mother spoke of had already belonged to Jack.

Rolling over, turning away from Sarah, he dropped his head deep in the pillow and was almost asleep when she said, "Why did you marry me, George?"

"What?" He lifted his head from the pillow, not turning to look at her.

"Do you love me George?"

His head dropped back on the pillow. "Of course, that's why we married."

"But that was planned."

"There's a sense of certainty when your life is planned. I'm sure you agree," he said. "We've had a long day, you should be tired. We leave early tomorrow morning for

Cape Cod, now get some sleep."

Yes, Cape Cod. Fond memories resided there. Would she bring more with her? The Wescotts had a summer home in Hyannis, seventy miles southeast of Boston. Every summer of her youth was spent at their large colonial home on Nantucket Sound. On occasion her father took her sailing when he wasn't working, but then he was always working. No different than Boston and he was endlessly on the phone, demanding something from some employee or business acquaintance.

Still turned away, George nestled his head more comfortably in the pillow while pulling the covers closer to his neck.

She looked at George, listening to his heavy breathing. This day was supposed to be the happiest of her life, yet she was miserable. She liked George, and even thought she loved him, but it was glorious being with Jack. He showed her the truth in being a woman. Now it was forever written on her heart, no other man could take Jack's place.

Throwing on her nightgown, she stepped out onto the balcony that overlooked the garden. It seemed like an Indian summer, so warm with no hint of a breeze. Faint voices of the last departing guests, floated up to the balcony, appearing unable to say goodbye to a festive day.

With night falling over the garden, the stars began to appear, twinkling, emitting their luminosity. The sweet smell of the flowers filling the garden for the celebration, seemed sharpened by the oncoming night air. The moon began to show its face, high in the sky, casting a flood of shadowy light across the garden. Would she ever see Jack again? And if so, would he remember her as she would remember him?

Smiling, her thoughts reflected back to New York…the hotdog…and yes…his song of Iowa. Pure enjoyment of the simple things of life. *What else is there?* She knew him for one day, yet she knew him all her life. *No one like him. No one.*

How could she have told her father, the heart knows no logic. And why should Jack's background matter? Does his humble beginnings make him less worthy, that he has less of a soul? Her father wasn't listening, he made her feel ashamed. Why? There's no shame in love.

How does she tell a soldier he was denied her love? What words could she have formed differently to tell him it was never to be? How lonely it must have been for him. No one to bid him farewell…come back safe…his girl would be waiting…that her love goes with him.

She could have defied her father, but Jack was going off to war. Where would she go? What knowledge did she have of the outside world, how it really worked? Her father made her feel scared to be with Jack, when she was afraid to be without him. Nothing made sense unless she was with him.

Then suddenly everyone lingering in the garden was gone. The last goodbyes were said. Quiet fell over the garden, except for the night sound of crickets deep in the garden beds, their song rising to fill the night.

She looked up at the sky, searching for the North Star. There it was, shining brighter than any star. She pointed to it as if Jack was guiding her hand, as he did on the balcony suite of the Le Grand Chateau Hotel.

You are somewhere under that star Jack Karsen. Be safe. I love you wherever you are. I love you.

Chapter 16

Sitting on the edge of his cot in the wood barracks at the Royal Air Force Alconbury station near Huntingdon, England, Jack flipped through the pages of the Boston Globe. He was just about to throw the newspaper on the floor when he noticed a wedding photo of Sarah and her betrothed in the society section…

…Boston society couple married. Sarah Wescott, daughter of Charlotte and Winston Wescott, the nation's richest investment tycoon marries George Minton, son of Ellen and Bradford Minton, shipbuilding magnate…

…It was unexpected, but then, what was he hoping? *Think of it Jack…the ring…the telegram. It said it all,* he told himself. But then he couldn't help thinking what form of fate brought them together at the precise moment, only to be torn apart? Or was it a chance meeting, a random event of which fate took no part? Maybe it was better this way. He had no right to ask her to wait for him. He may be gone a very long time, and may not survive the war.

Gordon Frazer, one of the B-17 pilots, left his cot and walked over to Jack. Clearly, he was Irish with a flash of red hair, light green eyes and his complexion speckled with freckles. A cigarette pack was stuffed into one rolled up sleeve of his white T-shirt, and a single cigarette was tucked behind his ear, ready for an immediate smoke. He came up behind Jack, leaned over Jack's shoulder and looked at what Jack was focusing so intensely on. Then he reached over Jack's shoulder, and pointed at the newspaper photo.

"Is that the girl?" Gordon wanted to know.

Jack knew what was coming. Gordon was not a man of few words, and seldom refrained from saying exactly what was on his mind. One would think it would get him into trouble, but he was lucky that way.

They met the first day in pilots' training and hit it off, becoming good friends, and like Jack, Gordon came from humble beginnings. His father died from the long term effects of exposure to mustard gas suffered in the trenches during World War I. His mother died shortly thereafter, and as an only child with no living relatives, Gordon spent most of his early life in an orphanage in New Jersey. Wanting to get into the war—perhaps in his blood—a bomber pilot appealed to Gordon rather than suffer the grim reality of ground combat like his father. At the orphanage, there was a lone piano no one seemed to care about. It found a home with Gordon. He could play a hell of a tune, couldn't read a note of music, played by ear.

"Yes, Gordon she's the girl," Jack said sadly. He threw the newspaper on the floor and moved to the head of his cot, leaning against the wall. His dog tags clicked together against his white T-shirt as he pushed the pillow to a comfort level behind his back. It was free time to relax. It was a tough business, war. Death a daily occurrence.

Gordon sat down on the edge of Jack's cot, picked up the newspaper off the floor and read the caption under the photo.

"Holy cow, Jack, she's a Brahmin."

"Brahmin?"

"Oldest and wealthiest New England families. Old Boston gentry, they're called."

Now Jack realized what the clerk at the Le Grand Chateau Hotel meant. Jack knew so little about her, just that she had said, "Boston. Founding fathers. Steep in history. Only child."

"You would have to get serious over the impossible, Jack. Plenty of girls out there and you had to pick society. What were you thinking?"

"I didn't plan it."

"Well, get over it."

"Over it?" Look of doom crossed Jack's face.

"Don't you get it, Jack? She's Boston, you're Iowa. It was just a fling."

"I can't believe that."

"I hate to say this Jack, but the photo speaks for itself."

"It was different. I know it." He couldn't get it out of his head that she loved him and class distinction had nothing to do with love.

Gordon just shook his head. Apparently, Jack wasn't listening.

"Ever feel this way, Gordon?"

"Yeah, I've felt that way. Sweet and sorrowful." Gordon told Jack what he's in for. "Giving your heart comes at a cost, Jack. Look what you're going through and the sweetness was only one day, and the rest, well, you got the message. I've been there and I don't like it. No one's going to tie me to their apron strings. I play the field."

Gordon's advice still didn't seem to do the trick. No help for Jack's grieving heart.

"Come on Jack, you've been breaking your heart over this girl long enough. It was one night, she's forgotten about."

"You don't understand. Everything about her is fine. She has grace, and most of all, she listens, feels what you say."

"Let it go, Jack, she's married."

Chapter 17

Any chance Jack would be coming home soon was suddenly dashed by America's unexpected entry into the war.

In the evening of December 9, 1941, Charlotte and Winston joined Sarah and George in the family room on the third floor of the Wescott mansion. U.S. President Franklin Delano Roosevelt was about to address the nation. Winston had made it known to family and close friends that he liked Roosevelt, because he was a Brahmin and Winston gave most generously to Roosevelt's campaign, even when he didn't believe entirely in his policies.

Winston checked his watch, pulling it by the long chain from his vest pocket. It was time. He turned on the radio...

…"On December 7th 1941, a date which will live in infamy…" the President's voice began, "…the United States of America was suddenly and deliberately attacked by naval and air forces of the Empire of Japan…We are now in this war. We are all in it…Every single man, woman and child is a partner in the most tremendous undertaking in our American history…It will not only be a long war, but it will be a hard war…in the difficult hours of the day…through dark days that may be yet to come…the human race are on our side. Many of them are fighting with us. All of them are praying for us…our hope and their hope for liberty under God."…

…When the President's speech had concluded, Winston who stood by the window, walked over and turned off the radio. What America feared most and wanted least had become reality. U.S. neutrality was over whether the American people wanted it or not. World War I—so named the war to end all wars—was not the end. It looked grim and the future unsure for America. It wouldn't be a white Christmas this year, but a bleak one.

Charlotte sat in a wingback chair, a ball of yarn in her lap. Knitting needles worked away in her hands, the woven yarn growing long against her legs. Winston had nervously chomped on his cigar during the President's speech, filling the room with smoke. His mind appeared to be running at full throttle, how he could financially benefit from the war, and how Bradford's furnaces would burn well into the nights. Forge more steel. More ships.

Standing by the radio, Winston looked at Charlotte still knitting away, her eyes glued on her creation.

"Charlotte," he said to draw her attention away from her labor he most likely thought dull.

As Charlotte looked up, her hands still working away, Winston gave her a look indicating it was time to retire. It appeared she knew what he meant. His baser instincts had come alive.

"It's time to say goodnight, Charlotte." Winston told her and with no emotion on her face, Charlotte set her knitting in a basket on the floor beside the chair. She was bound to obligate her husband in this and all things. Head of the household was never questioned. She and Winston bid their goodnight to George and Sarah and returned to the second floor and their apartment.

Sarah lay across a sofa, resting herself and George in an armchair nearby, continued to read his book, picking up where he left off before the President's address. It was hard to understand George. He was so quiet, purposely self-composed, and emotionally guarded. She had yet to witness strong passion in his voice, only politeness. Seldom did he kiss her and when he did, it was mainly on the cheek or forehead, rarely on the lips. Affection was assumed and not displayed. He was there and she was there.

They never lay together like she did with Jack, touching, feeling, the warmth of their bodies pressing. She and George didn't even sleep in the same bedroom, not since their wedding night. He only came to her when the urge moved him, and still there was no passion. It appeared as if it was a bothersome chore. It was evident their wedding night had been a prelude of what was to come, a life lived in emptiness. He was what her family had wanted for her, to live a life they deemed her calling. To have everything, yet have nothing? She watched her mother move at the instant command of her father. Was she to live her mother's life when she had hoped it would be different?

George couldn't help who he was, conditioned by his upbringing. It was the only way he knew how love was conducted—sterile, like a surgical procedure. Sometimes when George talked to her, he doesn't even see her. Perhaps, because he never spoke from depth of his heart, didn't know how. He was in this marriage as a devoted husband as he defined one to be, but for her, it was a marriage of convenience and loneliness. True loneliness has but one friend—love. She wondered if Jack was as lonely or had he found refuge in the arms of an English girl?

Oh, why couldn't she end her season of darkness? She wasn't alive without Jack, her very soul seemed lost. He taught her heart to sing and without him there was no song. Was knowing Jack a blessing or a curse?

She looked at George sitting in the wingback chair, saying nothing, the book still stuffed in his hands. The glow of the fire rose high in the fireplace behind him. *Living with George and in love with a soldier whose fate is unknown,* ran through her mind.

She felt a flutter in her womb, and placed her hand there. The baby would come in the spring, a mere three months. Perhaps then she could forget and let Jack go. A new life could mean a new beginning.

1942

Chapter 18

"No…no," Winston Wescott leaned over the side of the bed and shook his head. Then he moved closer, squinting at the newborn in Sarah's arms. "He doesn't look like anyone in the family," Winston said. Then he looked at George standing quietly at the foot of the bed who appeared deep in thought.

"How about a Minton?" Winston questioned George.

George cast a suspicious eye toward Sarah, yet he had nothing concrete in which to base his suspicion. He always appeared to think a lot before giving an answer or comment. He mostly agreed rather than deal with confrontation. If his answer was no, he remained quiet, appearing to ignore the question. A man of few words left one wondering what he was actually thinking.

Sarah's mind was more on the fact that the baby looked just like Jack—dark hair and hazel eyes—than their discussion about who the baby resembled. Now she would never forget Jack. He had left his footprint forever on her heart, and now on her daily life.

George was about to answer Winston's question when Charlotte piped in, "Babies don't look very much like anyone when they're born, Winston." She patted him gently on the back. Enjoy the moment, she seemed to be telling him, and try not to analyze everything. Although

Sarah knew Charlotte would never tell him that. It was not Charlotte's place to criticize her husband even in private.

Charlotte straightened the pillow behind Sarah's back in an apparent attempt to comfort her. Charlotte seemed relieved. The labor had been long and difficult, but the first baby usually is, Charlotte had told her. Winston, Charlotte and George had waited in the adjoining sitting-room, and when they heard the cry of new life, they simultaneously leaped from their chairs, smiles forming on their faces.

Charlotte finished fussing over Sarah, and went to open the French doors leading to the balcony overlooking the garden. She threw open the doors to let the spring air circulate into the stuffy room. The trees were bursting with blossoms, and the birds were singing sweet sounds in a spring season like never before. What a happy day for Charlotte. Generations of Wescotts had been born in the Wescott mansion. It was the tradition since the mansion was built and now, a new generation would carry on the Wescott heritage.

Charlotte took a deep breath, filling her lungs with the fresh spring air, a smile on her face. It seemed she couldn't imagine a lovelier spring bringing forth new life and a new birth. Then she returned to Winston still attempting to determine who the baby resembled.

"Well, he's got to look like someone." Winston pressed for an answer. He looked at Sarah as if she had the answer, but it appeared she was of no help.

Then George saved the day, but looked as if he didn't entirely retire his suspicion.

"I don't wish to disagree with you Winston," George said politely, "but Charlotte may be is right. We have a long line of ancestors that some of their features may have come to light."

Sarah looked at George as he spoke, his eyes still glued on her. She knew he wanted to put the debate to rest. That much Sarah gave him credit for. Winston was not easily deterred in his thinking. Once Winston had his mind on something, it was difficult for him to let go. So George standing up to her father no matter how polite his words were formed, he appeared to have some backbone.

No matter. Let them continue in their attempt to figure out who in the family's past the baby looked like. She was certain her father or mother would never have divulged a hint of her meeting Jack. Or even if it became known, the New York trip was nothing other than an unconsummated encounter with a soldier. They were forever honorably and faithfully committed to their long standing reputation, and would sacrifice anything for it.

Besides they had never seen Jack, never cared to ask his name and he was never spoken of again as if he never existed. So there should be no question the baby was anyone's but George's seed. So let their suspicious minds run rampant. Let them think what they want.

"Bradford and I thought Philip would be a good family name after my father," Winston said firmly. If he didn't have a son of his own to carry on the Wescott name, his grandson would bear a family name.

"Alright, Winston," Charlotte calmed him, his over excitement apparent.

George agreed. Even if he didn't approve, he really had no say in the matter. He couldn't win against the strength of both families.

"Philip Wescott Minton." Sarah announced and her words ended any further discussion. The baby's name didn't matter. He was Jack in her arms. She looked at his little face, his tiny arm stretched out to her, his hand opened wide. Sarah offered her little finger and he clasped it tightly as if Jack somewhere was holding onto her heart. She pulled the dearest, most precious child close to her breast. All her own. Just as Jack had been her own for one night, his child would be hers for all her life.

"Come Winston, let's go and let Sarah rest. Enough excitement has been created." Charlotte coaxed a grumbling Winston out of the room, retiring to their apartment on the second floor.

George moved to the other side of the bed next to Sarah and stood there, staring at her. "Is there something I need to know?"

She gave him a curious look. "I don't understand, George." She could have told him that she was naive, foolish, a brief affair that meant nothing when it meant everything. No good would come of it if he knew the truth. It was better to continue to live a lie—an unspoken truth. If it should become known, it would be a scar on the family's reputation. In that, her father was right. No word of her time in New York would be spoken in or outside the family. It would have to remain a secret. A secret is only a secret if it never leaves the lips.

George dismissed what he had asked Sarah and said, "Of course you would tell me."

1943

Chapter 19

Jack entered the base commander's headquarters at Horham Airbase, in Suffolk, England, closing the door behind him. He was tired, face drawn, dark circles under his eyes. The war had aged him.

Since America entered the war in the fight for freedom, American air and ground forces had been thrust heavily into the conflict. It was a hard war, the losses great and the end nowhere in sight.

The colonel, tall and well-fit for a man in his fifties, sat on a simple wooden chair behind a nondescript desk, the only furniture in the room besides a couple of large metal filing cabinets. Chairs on the other side of the desk to accommodate visitors were not a priority. No time for even simple conversation. Conducting the business of war took precedence. Plain and straightforward. State your business, get to the point, and fight a war.

In his flight suit, Jack stood at attention in front of the colonel and saluted his superior. "You sent for me, colonel sir?"

"At ease, lieutenant," the colonel instructed and Jack relaxed his stance, folding his hands behind his back.

The colonel rose from his chair and stood behind his desk in a well pressed everyday uniform of a long sleeve khaki shirt and pants, his status insignia pinned above his left breast pocket.

"You're one of the best bomber pilots, I have," the colonel pointed out, "if not the best in the bombardment group."

"Sir," Jack said, showing no emotion as to display humility at the compliment.

"Your assignment to a B-17 means you are flying a ten man weapon. When you are up there…" the colonel thrust his forefinger upward, "…you're not just the pilot, but an airplane commander responsible for the safety and efficiency of your crew. And that extends to twenty-four hours a day. You earn their respect, gain their confidence and trust, that's what makes a good B-17 commander. You must always be concerned with morale. Keep it high. They need to see strength. Unfaltering strength. If you've lost sense of this, I need to know."

"Sir, no disrespect, but are you trying to make a point here, sir?"

"I don't need to tell you, lieutenant, combat stress, fear and fatigue are a pilot's greatest enemy, and it must be dealt with for a pilot to be effective. I don't want you folding on me, lieutenant. We've got to win this damn war." The colonel warned Jack.

"Yes sir, I'm aware of that, sir."

"Are you lieutenant? Word came down that you're losing your focus."

"I don't know what you're referring to, colonel, sir."

"You came down hard, today, veered off the runway,

almost lost a wing. There isn't a damn thing wrong with your plane, lieutenant." The colonel laid it out as he saw it. In war, there was no time or place for error.

Losses were heavy that day. Four planes burned on landing, eight didn't return. Ten crew members in each, affecting the colonel as if every one of them was his own son. The colonel had seen too much death in two wars. The men on the base called him "an old war horse". His weathered face looked like railroad tracks, but he was smart and ran the base like he was running the war all by himself. He was no older than Jack when he volunteered for France as an aviator in the Lafayette Escadrille, the notorious French Flying Corp and faced the Red Baron. Few survived pitted against the most famous German World War I pilot. The colonel was the oldest man at the base, three years younger than Dwight Eisenhower, the war's first Supreme Allied Commander. Everyone at the base had considerable respect for the colonel. He knew his stuff.

"As base commander, there isn't a damn thing that happens around here or in fact…" he pointed upward again, "….up there that I don't know about. I'm as close to god as you're ever going to know. In fact, for your information, lieutenant, during this war, I am god."

"I understand, sir."

"Do you?" Then the colonel stated a quote: " 'These are the times that try men's souls…the harder the conflict, the more glorious the triumph…' Do you know who said that, lieutenant?"

"No sir, I don't."

"It is a timely statement by Thomas Paine, a political philosopher. The statement applied to the American Revolution and it applies now. The pressure of this war seems unforgiving for everyone. We all want to go home, but winning this war is paramount. The men look up to you, lieutenant. Need I say anymore?"

Chapter 20

Leaving the barracks, Gordon noticed Jack walking briskly toward the officers' club.

"Hey Jack," Gordon called. "Wait up."

Jack turned slightly, but didn't wait so Gordon ran to catch up.

"Hey, what's the hurry?" Gordon called.

"You need more push-ups Gordon," Jack commented when he noticed Gordon was out of breath for such a short run. "Sitting in that cockpit's got you soft."

"Soft? Getting in and out of the cockpit is all the exercise I need," Gordon said.

They entered the club and hung their leather jackets on a hook at the door, then headed for the bar. The bartender, a villager from the town of Horham, knew their usual, and when he saw them enter, had the drinks ready by the time Jack and Gordon sat down.

"What's on your mind, Gordon?" Gordon didn't let a moment go by if he could fight for some sort of justice in or out of the cockpit.

"I heard the old man had a talk with you today," Gordon said, referring to the colonel and Jack looked at him puzzled.

"Everyone knows what goes on around here," Gordon said. "I know what's eating you and it's getting to you big time, so much so, it's affecting your flying."

No answer from Jack.

"That girl, the newspaper photo in your pocket," Gordon said. "How you expect to get over her, I don't know. You've certainly had enough time."

"I don't talk about it so why do you?" Jack grabbed his drink and walked away.

Gordon followed Jack to the end of the bar and sat down next to him. "You want to kill yourself, take a gun to your head, but don't put your crew at risk. You fly like you're on a suicide mission."

"Hell, there all suicide missions. The men know it. Look, I got this crap from the colonel today, I don't need it from you, Gordon," Jack snapped.

Gordon understood that irritability, sudden temper flashes were common symptoms of the men under daily pressure, and worrying about things they can't control didn't help.

"She's still got you so tied up, you're in knots." Gordon jabbed his forefinger into the heart of Jack's flight suit as he said, "She there and deep."

"I can't get her out of my mind, and I can't get her out of there either. I feel like I'm flying without a map." The summer of 1941 would never let him go.

"Yeah, love is its own suicide mission," Gordon said, almost as an afterthought, staring at nothing. But then again, he had told that to Jack before. Not in equivalent words, but Jack got the message. "Look Jack, your nerves are shot. Hell, war is brutal. We need a break."

Jack stared at Gordon's wings over the left breast pocket of his flight suit, a reminder to all pilots to keep their mind on the war.

"I'm just edgy," Jack said.

"Sure, we're all working on adrenaline, Jack, in the cockpit, bombing every day. Let's use our forty-eight hour pass. A little R and R will put you back on course."

Chapter 21

Sarah entered the ward at Camp Edwards Convalescent Hospital on Cape Cod. The ward was full. Beds lined the wall on each side of the ward. Those of the recovering soldiers who were not resting in their beds were sitting in wheelchairs along the aisle. Once a month, Sarah spent a weekend at the Wescott summer home on Cape Cod so she could volunteer for the Red Cross. It was a way she could feel closer to Jack and maybe someone, somewhere in this war might be helping him.

A woman in her fifties wearing a white uniform, hat and shoes approached Sarah.

"Can you help with letters today? Some of the soldiers would like to write home," the nurse said, handing Sarah a pencil and paper. "Start with the young man in the wheelchair facing the open window."

Sarah looked to where the nurse pointed. The soldier was fair haired, that much she could tell by the back of his head above the wheelchair. She walked down the aisle toward the soldier, passing the wounded in hospital gowns, some heavily bandaged, some with missing limbs.

Two nurses were attending some of the wounded, attempting to make them comfortable. There were two other Red Cross volunteers on the ward floor, one changing bed sheets and the other attending a doctor making rounds. They were identifiable by their light blue cotton dress with a white collar and cuffs. A Red Cross patch was sewn on the left pocket and shoulder.

Sarah came up behind the soldier in the wheelchair who was staring intensely out the window where the sunlight streamed across his face and the ward. Perhaps he was lost somewhere where the terror of war didn't invade his thinking. Sarah placed her hand on the top of the wheelchair near his head, and leaned over to look into his face. He wasn't yet twenty years old.

"Hello soldier. I'm Sarah. What's your name?"

When the soldier heard her voice, he turned his face away from the open window, his grey eyes looking into hers.

"Hello," he said quietly.

Sarah moved around to the side of the wheelchair and noticed he had no legs. A blanket covered the lap of his hospital gown, falling to the floor. This scene was not new to her, but every time she saw war inflicted injuries, she had to draw every strength she had to be brave and cheerful, not show pity.

Sarah smiled to help him feel comfortable.

"I'm Andy," he said.

"I'm glad to meet you, Andy."

"You're a volunteer. I can tell by your uniform."

"Yes." She nodded. "Where are you from, Andy?"

"Missoula Montana."

"Beautiful country."

"You've been there?"

"No, but I have heard that it's great for fishing and hunting."

"There are great places for fly fishing, but Montana is like nowhere else in the country." He glanced down at his missing limbs hidden by the blanket. "I guess I won't be doing much of that anymore. I would like to go home. Nearly two years in the war is a long time to be away."

Sarah bit her lip to keep the tears away and quickly changed the subject.

"Would you like me to write a letter for you.? Someone at home perhaps?"

"I would appreciate that very much. I know my mom must be worried about me. I could do it myself—"

"It's alright, soldier. I'm glad to help." Sarah pulled a chair over and sat down next to him. She took up the pencil to begin. "Whenever you're ready, Andy."

"Dear mom," he began. "I'm doing alright, but mom, when you see me, please don't cry. I'm lucky. Other guys…well, they're not as well off. I don't regret it. I did what I had to do. I'm coming home. That's what you want more than anything. I love you mom."

Then suddenly he choked up, bursting into tears.

"I'm sorry, how can I help?" Sarah offered.

He wiped away his tears then with apparent pain in his voice he said, "He was in the trench right next to me, hungry for home when suddenly bullets started flying everywhere. A bullet went right through his head. I can't forget it," he sobbed. "I held him in my arms before I had to let him go."

Sarah fell silent. War was no place a mother wanted her son to be. Every day, living in fear, hoping the dreaded telegram wouldn't find her doorstep. And the small Service Flag with a blue star sewn in the center hanging in the front window of her home would change to gold.

Andy wiped his eyes and smiled, grateful for Sarah's help.

"I have a girl, you know," he said softly.

"She's waited for you all this time?"

"We were going to get married before I left."

"Then you should see her," Sarah said.

The soldier's smile quickly disappeared. A distant look came to his face. He turned away to look out the window at the peace, away from the war and what may awaited him back home.

Sarah couldn't imagine such courage. So many men with dreams and hopes for their future, taking up life in a different form than what they once knew, but not bitter about it.

She thought of George. He would not volunteer, go off to war, follow those who went of their own volition. It was not his style. Nor would he be drafted. He was certainly age qualified, but married men with wives and children were permitted deferment due to financial dependency. This was not the case with George, but the government didn't take into consideration his wealth. Besides, there were so many politicians Winston had lined pockets, that a simple phone call would have done the trick.

"Okay soldier, I'll post your letter today," she said, then thought of Jack. She gave freely of her time comforting the wounded, yet she never gave a final wave or a last glimpse of her to a soldier who may never return.

She started to leave, but Andy called to her.

"Wait, please. It's awfully nice of you to give your time."

Sarah smiled.

"Do you have someone in the war?" he inquired gently.

At first Sarah didn't know how to answer, thinking of Jack, but then she said, "Everyone knows someone serving in this war with so many giving willingly and courageously without question. Just like you, fighting for freedom. You're heroes."

"No..." he said reflecting, "...the men lying dead on the battlefield, they're the heroes."

***

Sarah went to the cafeteria and sat with Martha, another Red Cross volunteer Sarah had met the first day she arrived at the military hospital.

"I finally got a letter." Martha informed Sarah as she finished her sandwich. "He says things are tough. He's still flying a P-51 Mustang escort protecting the B-17 bombers. The harsh schedule is unrelenting, but I'm not to worry. He promises to be home and get married. We are going to buy a house and raise a family. He wants lots of children," she laughed. "I can't wait to cook his favorite meal."

Sarah listened to Martha bursting with joy over a treasured letter from her soldier and the thought of a humble life when the war was over with the man who would make it all worthwhile, uninhibited by social norms. Sarah felt she had found a friend and one she wanted to confide in.

How she wished she could tell Martha about Jack, but her father forbid her to speak of him and within the family, your word was bond and secured with honor. So they simply talked about everyday things, when the war would end and her soldier would come home.

Sadly though, when the war was over and their volunteer services would no longer be required, they would have to reluctantly say their goodbyes. She and Martha lived different lives. Winston would not permit friendship outside his circle of Upper-Class Bostonians.

Chapter 22

Sarah had heard so many stories that would make one's heart weep, unimaginable sorrow from the lips of the war wounded, that she had to find out where Jack was in the war and that he was safe. For any news of the fighting overseas, she like many Americans had to rely on newspapers, radio reports or news reels at movie theatres. Jack had been gone for two years. She had to end her need to know.

On her yearly June shopping trip to New York, she went directly to a local office of the U.S. War Department. It would not be wise to go to an office in Boston for fear she might be recognized, and questions would be asked. A woman in her position needed to be careful. People never forget. Upper-Class Boston was tight-knit. Once intimacy was revealed, it was always remembered and if the society news got hold of it, the slightest whisper would ruin her family.

Inside the lobby of the war department, she went straight to the information desk where an elderly woman was directing people to various parts of the building.

"Room 212," the woman told Sarah.

When Sarah reached Room 212, she felt nauseated and stood at the door to catch her breath. It must have been the steps to reach the second floor. Naturally, she would feel that way, she was pregnant. George's child. There was no question this time. She saw a drinking fountain a few steps away, and after refreshing herself, she made her way back to the door that would give her the answer she was seeking.

She entered a large room filled with the sound of fans whirling above, the clinking of typewriters keys, and the buzzing of voices. Employees sat at desks lining the room in rows. A chair was placed at the side of each desk, available for people who were inquiring about those fighting in the war. Sun streamed through the tall windows on one side of the room, adding the summer heat to the stifling room. Along the wall at the entry were chairs filled with waiting people.

A middle aged woman at the front desk saw Sarah enter. "Are you here to locate someone in the war?" the receptionist said when Sarah approached her desk.

"Yes, I am."

The receptionist handed Sarah a clip board. "Sign in, take a seat. You'll be called."

Sarah complied with the request, then found an empty chair next to a woman who was wearing a Gold Star pinned to her dress lapel which represented a loved one lost in the war. The honor no one wants.

"You may have to wait quite a while," the woman said softly.

"Have you been waiting long?" Sarah said.

"About an hour, but I don't mind if it helps me locate my other son. You see, I haven't heard from him in over a month. Mail is slow from the Front, and sometimes not at all."

"Your other son?"

"The war took one," the woman said sadly.

Sarah became quiet. *How many more must die?* She thought. *Sons lost, mothers weep.* What could she say to the woman inquiring about her son? Sarah wondered if Jack's mother wore a Gold Star.

If any good came from the war, amid the suffering and blood flowing immeasurably across Europe, Africa and the Pacific, the war had pulled America out of a suffering economy after the 1929 market crash. With thousands of men at war, women rolled up their sleeves, offered their strength and sweat to man assembly lines, build war materials—tanks, guns, planes, bombs. They served in uniform, driving trucks, repairing airplanes, nursing the wounded. Everyone unselfishly pitched in to do whatever was needed if it would bring their fighting men home.

Victory gardens were planted in backyards by families everywhere in America to help lower the price of vegetables needed for the troops. Winston had made it known, he was strongly opposed to turning up the soil at the Wescott mansion: "Digging up the lawn to plant seed is ridiculous…" he had said, "…I'll just buy more bonds, and that'll put an end to the discussion. After all, bonds are indeed an investment." And when Sarah was ready to do her part, however small, George, but mostly her father forbid it. Woman of Boston society did not work. A working married woman did so out of economic necessity.

Winston and Bradford were not without some sympathy for the war. They gave generously to the Red Cross, therefore why should she volunteer? But after much effort, she convinced her father and George that at least one member of the family should serve as a volunteer to defend freedom. She couldn't in all good conscience remain at home.

Her father was not one to easily give in, but times were changing. Women were coming into their own. "Opinionated," her father had told her. "Too big for their britches, forgetting their sex, their place in society. Pretty soon, they'll be wearing the pants." It appeared to Sarah, he blamed the war, and an independent attitude spawned from the war, but in essence he had no one to blame but himself. Sarah was very much like him and she knew he didn't like what he saw.

Sarah felt faint again. She had little breakfast and lunchtime was drawing near. She left her seat in Room 212 of the war department and went to the receptionist at the front desk.

"Do you think I can have some water?" Sarah said as she blotted the perspiration from her forehead with her handkerchief.

"Why yes, my dear." The receptionist instructed Sarah to sit in the chair beside her desk while she went to retrieve water.

Returning, the receptionist handed Sarah the water.

"How far along are you?" The receptionist appeared as if she knew, intuition was her guide. She had four of her own. She didn't wait for an answer and quickly turned to motion a male employee to allow Sarah to go to his desk.

"You go ahead, dear. Mr. Blanchet will see you."

"But it isn't fair, the others have waited so long," Sarah said.

The receptionist smiled. "They will understand. People are most tolerant and forgiving in these difficult times."

Sarah thanked her, then walked to the middle of the room and sat on the chair by Mr. Blanchet's desk. He looked like a kindly gentleman with a pleasant smile and warm eyes.

"How can I help you?" he said.

"I'm inquiring about a soldier, Lieutenant Jack Karsen."

"When was the last time you heard from Lieutenant Karsen?" he said, but Sarah had no answer to his question. Instead she said:

"All I know is he was going to England. Bomber pilot."

A surprised look crossed Blanchet's face. A bomber pilot was the most dangerous occupation of the war. Casualty rates were eighty-nine percent.

"You say…a bomber pilot?" he repeated to confirm.

"Yes."

"Are you a relative?"

"No."

"I'm sorry. If you are not related, I can't give out any information on military personnel."

"Please, every day, I check the dead or missing printed in the daily newspaper and his name is not listed. I just want to know if he's alright."

When he saw a sudden sadness cross Sarah's face, he seemed sorry for her. So many loved ones come to the war department, wanting to know of those sacrificing overseas, when no letters come from the Front. He appeared to notice the Red Cross Pin clasped to the collar of her dress.

"Are you a member of the Red Cross?"

"Volunteer," she said.

He looked around the room, discretely, to check if any of his co-workers were watching. Then quietly, almost in a whisper, he said, "Leave a number where you can be reached and I'll see what I can find."

Chapter 23

Leaving the war department, Sarah walked to the Le Grand Chateau Hotel. Passing St. Patrick's Cathedral, she decided to go inside. She wasn't Catholic, but she was sure that god, if there was one, wouldn't mind.

It was quite refreshing inside. The stone walls provided a comforting coolness from the warm day. She lit a candle by the saint called Andrew where she had read he was the saint of good will. Then she whispered a prayer for Jack…*keep him safe…bring him home.*

From St. Patrick's Cathedral, she walked to the hotdog stand where she and Jack once went on East 59th Street, and there was Harvey still manning the stand. There was no one ordering a hotdog at the moment, and she walked right up to the stand, a big smile on her face, happy to relive a memory.

"Hello Harvey."

He looked at her as if he was trying to recall. Then he said, "Oh yes, the soldier. You were with the soldier."

"Yes, I'm Sarah."

"How is he? Is he alright?"

"I think so."

"You two didn't get married."

"No," she replied and he didn't make further inquiries into the subject. It would appear to be intrusive. Instead he asked, "Can I get you a hotdog?"

"Sure, with everything on it." This time she intended to eat the whole dog.

Opening the steamer, the aroma filled the air, flooding her mind with sweet memories. He handed her the hotdog, and refused payment.

"Harvey, how are you going to make a living if you give your product away." Remembering that he refused payment from Jack.

"Let me tell you a secret," he said as he leaned over and whispered, "I only do it for pretty ladies."

Chapter 24

When Sarah heard the phone ringing in her room at the Le Grand Chateau Hotel, she rushed down the hall. She hurriedly slipped the key in the door. The radio was playing inside. The maid must have turned it on. The melody was a favorite war song by Mack Kay, *Goodbye Dear, I'll Be Back In a Year. Cause I'm in the Army Now….*

She switched it off. *War, war, war. A reminder everywhere,* she thought. *The last thought on your mind when you close your eyes at night, and the first thought opening them. Father had once said there will always be war. It's the natural state of man.*

She rushed to the phone, picked up the receiver.

"Hello Sarah, this is mother," came the voice on the other end.

"Oh, mother." *Not Mr. Blanchet.*

"You're out of breath. Are you alright?" Charlotte said.

"Yes, I'm quite alright."

"Philip misses you terribly. If he could just hear your voice, he might feel better." Charlotte handed the phone to Philip.

"Hello my little darling, Philip," Sarah said. "Mommy will be home day after tomorrow." She doubted he knew what she meant. Time was not a concept a fifteen month old could understand. "Give the phone to grandmother. I love you."

"He's such a sweet spirited child," Charlotte said. "I've never seen a child so sensitive."

Just like Jack, Sarah thought.

"But don't you worry, he'll be alright," Charlotte said. "You finish your shopping. It's about time you got away. It's been two years. You refuse to go last year when Philip was three months old."

"I know he's in good hands, mother. Goodbye."

Sarah hung up the phone. The instant she lifted her hand from the receiver, the phone rang again.

"Sarah Minton?" The man's voice said.

"Yes."

"This is Mr. Blanchet from the war department. I have the information concerning your inquiry of Lieutenant Jack Karsen. He's still in England. He was with the RAF Bomber Command initially, but when America entered the war, he moved to the 8th American Air Force, 95th Bomb Group, 336th Bombardment Squadron."

She grabbed a hotel pen and pad of paper and quickly jotted down the information.

"He's stationed at Horham Airbase, Station 119 in the County of Suffolk, England," Blanchet said. "You can address correspondence to him at that airbase, but I'm sure you know by now it's hard to get mail overseas with our ships under siege in the Atlantic."

"Thank you, Mr. Blanchet." She said goodbye and hung up. She breathed a sigh of relief. Jack was safe, for now. Then she wrestled with her thoughts. What was she thinking? She was carrying one man's child and in love with another. But then she reasoned, she may hold George's child in her body, but she would never be free from Jack. In Philip's eyes, there was Jack.

Chapter 25

Music played on the radio in the jeep as it bumped along the road heading toward London. It was an hour drive to the city from the airbase. Gordon drove, said he knew the way.

Gordon stuffed a cigarette in his mouth. Lighting it, he inhaled heavily, the tip burning red, the smoke leaving his lips in a long white stream. Then he started humming to the tune on the radio. Gordon had a descent voice so why wasn't he singing? Jack sat back as Gordon kept beat to the music, tapping his forefinger on the steering wheel.

Entering the city, very little of London had been spared the German bomb. Shells of buildings stood ghostly in a sea of rubble. Everything appeared black with shades of gray. The sun didn't exist, hidden behind a thick veil of perpetual smoke. The city burned by night into day. The Germans had been beating the hell out of all England for three years, instilling terror in the hearts of the British people. It was Hitler's insane plan meant to force Britain to negotiate and accept peace or he would erase England from the face of the earth.

Jack took his hat off, letting the wind find its way through his hair then he pushed back his hair with his hand, and stuffed the hat back on his head.

"Do you know where this night club is?" Jack asked

Gordon.

"One of the men said it's on Leicester Square."

"Leicester Square," Jack repeated, "do they even have street signs anymore in this hellhole?"

"If we can drop a bomb into a pickle barrel, we'll find it." Then in the next breath, Gordon said. "Hey, this must be the place." He noticed a dilapidated sign over a building, darkened with bomb dust. "400 Club. Just as described at the airbase."

Gordon pulled up in front and turned off the ignition. "There's only about four clubs in London, but this is the best." He hopped out of the jeep.

"Doesn't look like much. Might be better inside," Jack said.

"It sure as hell will be better." Gordon glanced around at London. "Looks like we landed on the moon. Let's get inside. It's considered dangerous in London after dusk."

"Dangerous? You have to be kidding, Gordon."

They laughed.

"Hey buddy, are you just going to sit in the jeep?" Gordon said, and Jack sensed Gordon wasn't interested in wasting time. Who knows whether their next flight over Germany would be their last. It was a chance to live without the war.

Jack slid out of the jeep, walked around to Gordon.

"Nice to wear our uniform for a change." Gordon gave Jack a friendly slap on the back as they entered the club.

It could have been any club, it was undistinguishable,

but it was stepping into a different world than the perils of death existing outside. Heavy black curtains covered the windows to prevent light from escaping into the night—easy target for German bombs. There was a small band in the back of the club. Tables lining each side of a dance floor were filled with military men of all ranks stationed from airbases in Britain. English women were sitting with them socializing, while others were dancing with military, attempting to forget the war.

Two women chatting at a table with some military and other women noticed Jack and Gordon settle themselves at a table on the other side of the dance floor. The women walked over to introduce themselves.

Gordon poked Jack to get his attention when he caught sight of the two women headed their way, welcoming smiles on their faces. Gordon slapped a wide smile on his face—just his type, a blonde and a brunette, young and attractive. Gordon must have been in glory, he was definitely looking for action. He had once said women flocked to him, because they couldn't resist running their fingers through his flaming hair and of course, his charm.

"They may not be French girls, but I hear they're just as much fun," Gordon hoped, turning to regard Jack.

Jack smiled. *Gordon forever the Romeo.*

Like gentlemen, Jack and Gordon rose from their chairs to greet them.

"Can we join you, soldiers?" One of the women said.

"Sure." Gordon happily accepted.

"I'm Myrtle and this is Joan."

"Hello." Joan said.

"Gordon and Jack," Gordon introduced and Jack nodded, smiling.

The women sat down at the plain wooden table. No fancy table cloth like the Saint-Veran restaurant.

"You're both American." Myrtle could tell by Gordon's accent.

"Pilots," Gordon told them.

"First time Joan or I have seen pilots and very few soldiers anymore." Myrtle joked and Gordon and Jack laughed as there was nothing but military in the club.

"Naturally, they don't come around anymore. Too much danger here." Joan added to the joke, and there was laughter again.

"I hear you pilots are bombing Germany, but what can you do to help London?" Joan said. "The Nazis are bombing poor London into oblivion. You can't get clothing and very little food. Nobody knows what's going to happen. People are scared to death, huddled in air raid shelters, sometimes all night."

"There isn't too much more left of London," Myrtle said. "We're going to have to dig ourselves out of this grave for years."

Jack looked at Gordon's face. Gordon had made it known, no more war talk—forty-eight hours to get as far away from the cockpit as he could. No doubt Gordon needed to change the subject.

"Can we buy you girls a drink?" Gordon pulled his

chair close to Joan. It was obvious Gordon favored dark hair ladies. Brunettes dominated the photos on the table by his cot.

"Gee that's swell fellas. We can only get scotch. The war you know," Myrtle said.

"Same as the base," Gordon said. "That's fine with me, and its Jack's preferred drink."

"What do you say we dance?" Joan urged Gordon.

"Sure Joan. Could you take care of the drinks, Jack?"

"Will do," Jack said.

While the waitress appeared at the table, and took the order, Joan and Gordon walked to the dance floor and joined in with the other couples.

Sitting at the table next to Jack, Myrtle reached for his hand. "Would you like to dance?"

He pulled his hand away. "I'm not really a dancer."

"Okay, then we'll just sit and chat." It appeared to her that small talk might bring him to relax a bit. Pilots were always uptight. Living the war every day, it was probably hard to think of anything else.

Myrtle didn't notice the waitress bring their order, then leave. She just kept staring at Jack, looking as if she was trying to figure him out.

"I think a pilot is the dreamyist guy," Myrtle went on. "How long are you going to be in London, Jack? Maybe we could get together again."

Jack didn't answer. He took a couple of hard swallows of scotch as he watched Gordon and Joan on the dance floor, chatting, laughing, bringing back moments of the

Saint-Veran restaurant before the war. His hand squeezed his half empty glass as if he could never let go of the cockpit wheel.

"So what's it like up there?" Myrtle nonchalantly pointed upward. With still no response from Jack, it appeared to her that Jack wasn't listening, probably as sick of the war as she was. But what else is there to talk about? At least the volume of the music would muffle the sound of the bombs which would soon own the night.

On the dance floor, the band began playing Irving Berlin's, *Be Careful It's My Heart* as Gordon and Joan stepped lightly to the music.

"What's wrong with your friend?" Joan said. "He appears quiet.

"Girl back home," Gordon said. "He can't seem to shake it."

"Oh, one of those."

Gordon nodded. "She's got ahold of his soul."

"Too bad."

"Doesn't even have her photo, just some clipping he pulled out of a newspaper, and tucked it in his pocket. He looks at it often, seems to give him strength."

"Do you think she'll be waiting for him when he gets back?" Joan said.

"Not this one."

On the other side of the room, Myrtle slid her chair closer to Jack. He didn't talk much, not the fun loving spirit she seemed to have known with other soldiers. Change the subject. Maybe he'll loosen up.

"Where are you from, Jack?"

"Iowa." Jack's hand clasped the glass tighter.

"Oh, I thought you'd be from California where all the movie stars live. You know I'd like to get into the movies, if this damn war ever gets over." Myrtle kept talking about anything and everything…on…and on…mostly about Hollywood, and that she imagined herself as the love interest in movies with major stars who she rattled off their names as if she was reading a laundry list.

A vocalist sitting among the band members, rose from her chair, stepped to the microphone and with a sweet voice began to sing…

After the war is over,
And you're in my arms again,
I'll whisper that I love you,
I just don't know where or when,

After the war is over,
After the parting's done,
We'll be together forever,
And always be as one,

I speak your name,
In my dreams,
And you come to me,
With a love so divine,
It was meant to be,

In my heart,
You will remain,
And forever be,
The only one for me,

After the war is over,
And you're in my arms again,
I'll whisper that I love you,
I just don't know where or when,

…Myrtle's voice droned on in the background as the music and lyrics flowed through the room, forcing the storm to rage back into Jack's dying heart while images of Sarah took hold of his mind. Seemed as if god and the devil were at odds within him. There was no escape. He was committed to one woman to his last breath of life.

Jack turned to Myrtle and said, "You seem like a nice girl, and I'm sure you'll find someone. But not me."

Alone, Jack walked out of the club into the night, and with him flowed the music and lyrics…

After the war is over,
After the parting's done,
We'll be together forever,
And always be as one.

Chapter 26

Dear Jack,

You have a son…we have a son…ours…

…Sarah began to write then hesitated. She lifted the pen to look at the envelope yet to be addressed, lying on the desk next to her words.

It was like all the other letters she began and couldn't finish, but there was some comfort in the exercise for nothing else existed when her pen touched the paper. She was away from her world and with him.

She rested her pen on the desk, and looked out the windows of the French doors leading to the balcony of her sitting-room. Snow covered the garden in a blanket of pure white. Glazed frost lay heavy on the tree branches dark against the grim sky. Icicles hung long and thick along the balcony railing. A howling wind blew across the garden, and battered against the windows. With the thought of the war still raging in three parts of the globe, the gray of winter seemed colder, darker.

Would the stroke of a pen change her life or was her life like the seasons that "…dance to the mysterious tune, intoned in the distance by an invisible piper."?

Lifting the piece of fine linen stationery with the engraved initials *SWM* from her desk, she walked to the stone fireplace. The fire was burning steadily through the wood, the flames reaching high. She held the letter over the fire then released it, letting the flames consume her words, the ashes rising to find their way to the heavens.

Maybe someday, there will be a chance to tell him. Someday.

Chapter 27

Gordon marched into the officers' club, looking for Jack. Most of the men had retired to their barracks, but for a few men dragging out the night hours. The officers' club was always open to accommodate men who were unable to sleep due to a heightened state of alertness from a bombing run, or who had difficulty forgetting the day's memories—what went wrong?

There was a card game in the back of the room with a table of men chomping cigars. The radio was playing in the background and a few men from Jack's crew were swinging around the floor, dancing the jitterbug to Prince and Raye's, *Boogie Woogie Bugle Boy of Company 'B'*. The everyday flight schedule was rough and it had not changed—six to nine hours in the air, seven days a week so seldom were any of the men on the base out of their flight suits.

When Gordon entered, pushing past the men kicking up their heels, two of Jack's crew members, stopped dancing to address Gordon's interruption.

"Hey Gordon, you're messing up our dance," Bob said.

"Come join us," Mike added.

"Wait until you get leave, dance with the women." Gordon called back as he headed straight for the bar and

Jack nursing a drink.

"We're practicing to impress the women when we get our leave," Mike said.

"You men have had too much to drink," Gordon said.

"What are you talking about? We're not old enough to drink," Bob said.

"Yeah, not old enough to drink, but man enough to fight a war. How does that work?" One of the other men on the dance floor commented.

Gordon just ignored the men.

"Ah, let him go," Mike said, waving his hand in the air, dismissing the issue, resuming the dance.

Sitting at the bar, Jack heard the exchange between Gordon and the men, and watched Gordon heading his way, moving with strong purpose.

Jack gulped down what remained of his scotch whiskey and was ready to retire to the barracks when Gordon appeared at his side.

"So, are you getting out of this war?" Gordon came right to the point.

"No, I've signed up again."

"So, it's true." Gordon had heard men in the barracks, talking to the contrary.

Jack didn't reply. He didn't want to get into a confrontation with Gordon. Gordon, in Jack's opinion, always appeared to take Jack under his wing, thinking again he knew what was best for him.

"Why did you do that, Jack?"

"What are you talking about?"

"Signing up for another tour. What the hell do you think I'm talking about? You flew your twenty-five missions and more. Hell, more than I have. You're done." Gordon could have told him the survival rate was six missions, but Jack knew. "Go home. Get the hell out of this insanity. Find that girl, tell her you love her."

"She's married. You reminded me. Besides the war needs all the pilots they can get, Gordon."

"You're tempting fate."

"Pushing my luck?"

"Call it what you want. Targets are getting tougher. Odds are not good."

Jack shook his head no. "You know Gordon, it's hard to find replacements as fast as we're losing them. Besides, I'm not good at anything else right now, except flying that heavy piece of machinery, and I can't leave my crew. If I'm going to go, this is the way. Something that gives life meaning. Anyway, there's no reason for me to go back home."

Suddenly the music playing on the radio was interrupted…

…"Ladies and gentlemen…" the voice on the radio began, "…to lift the morale of our fighting men and those at home, we give you the timeless words of England's Prime Minister Winston Churchill."…

…The men in the officers' club became quiet. The men on the dance floor gathered around the radio as

Churchill spoke of defending the British island and it would never surrender.

When Churchill's speech was over, the music began again, and all the men in the officers' club went back to their entertainment.

Still sitting at the bar next to Jack, Gordon pulled his pack of cigarettes from his breast pocket—now rationed at home, but free to soldiers—and noticed the pack was empty. Crushing it with his hand, he tossed it to the bartender who caught it on the fly.

"What, no more cigarettes?" Jack said. Gordon always had a backup.

"Giving them up for the war effort. That's my contribution."

Jack smiled.

"Do you think they will ever give up?" Gordon said. "The Germans I mean."

"Well, we won't." Jack was sure of it.

JUNE 5, 1944
One day before the invasion of Normandy
(D-Day)

Chapter 28

The day's bombing routine was scheduled like any other mission. The B-17 Flying Fortress bombers and single-seat escort fighter planes from several Allied airbases inside and outside England, met up over the North Sea, and headed southeast to their bombing target deep inside Germany. But today's military operation was significantly larger than Jack had ever witnessed before.

From the cockpit windows of Jack's B-17 bomber, flew an armada of hundreds and hundreds of B-17s and American P-51 Mustangs and British Spitfires stretching as far as the eye could see and beyond—V formations stacked tight at twenty-four, twenty-five and twenty-six thousand feet above the earth. Each B-17 and escort plane had a personal marking painted on its nose—name or picture the individual men were proud of, and believed protected them, a good luck symbol. Jack's crew chose *Fly for Freedom.*

Twenty-four, seven the Allies bombed Germany—the British by night and the Americans by day—but this armada was an extraordinary show of strength. Something big was about to happen…

…"Tomorrow morning gentlemen, we will launch the deepest bombing raid against Germany since the war began," the base commander announced, addressing the airmen gathered at the briefing in a Quonset hut the night before.

He stepped aside to reveal a giant map of Central Europe on the wall behind him. Pushpins marked the mission's targets. A red tape ran from the European Allied airbases across the North Sea into Germany and to the big B—Berlin—the hunting ground of the Luftwaffe—German Air Force.

"Men…" he said to the pilots and crew members sitting on long benches, facing him, "…what you see here on this map…" he continued, using a long wooden pointer. "…you have never seen before. Bombers and fighter escort planes from every Allied airbase will be in the air. Bombers will hit enemy airbases, assembly plants, aircraft factories, supply lines, oil refineries, railroad yards, and yes, the city of Berlin. This is unrestrictive bombing. All targets are onboard. Destroy Germany's ability to wage war, and bring Hitler to his knees.

"In essence we are going to bomb the hell out of Germany. Pound the rubble to dust, and send the Third Reich to hell," the base commander said, stressing the point. "Men, you must make every bomb count." He set the pointer down on a side table. "Be aware, the fighter escorts will be with the bombers as long as possible. In other words, escorts will protect the bombers from the German Luftwaffe going in, but on the way out, bombers may be on their own.

"What we do tomorrow, June 5, 1944, will set the

stage in determining the end of this god damn war in Europe. Gentlemen the day of the Lord is at hand." Then he paused, looked straight in the eyes of the men sitting before him. "Say goodbye to the man sitting next to you—he's not going home."

A deadening silence fell over the Quonset hut. No one turned to look. No one flinched. By the massive amount of targets indicated on the map and the tone of the base commander's voice, the men sensed it.

Most of those men at the briefing were mainly nineteen and twenty year olds sent into the most hostile skies of Germany. Few had ever been in an airplane before the war, some as tender as sixteen and hardly men as the base commander had addressed them. But surely they were men to have guts enough to fight a god awful war where the attrition rate was high and fast. Mounting casualties warranted training to be lowered from six weeks to sixteen days. War waits for no one…

…There were ten crew members in each one of the hundreds of B-17 bombers flying in formation outside the cockpit windows of Jack's B-17 bomber. Many headed for certain death. Of Jack's own crew, none had ever left their home state before—Arthur the Tail Gunner from Georgia; Steve and Dave Waist Gunners, brothers from Illinois; Earl the Radio Operator/Top Gunner from Missouri; Mike the Bombardier/Nose Gunner from California; Charlie the Navigator/Nose Gunner from Tennessee; Bob the Engineer/Top Gunner from Jack's home town in Iowa; and Joe the Ball Turret Gunner from Florida. And then there was Jack's co-pilot Martin from Texas who was smarter than any man Jack knew. Martin loved to stand on a crate in the officers' club as if it was a stage and recite Shakespeare's Macbeth while Gordon played a line of music here and there on the piano to add to the drama. Tired of hearing it, the men in the officers' club threw ice cubes or anything they could find at Martin to silence him. They grew to know Macbeth by heart.

Thirty to forty men lived in a barracks so they got to know each other like brothers. *A pilot stood next to you one day*...Jack thought...*and the next day, he's gone. No one has to tell you. You just see his cot folded over on his bed. Worse thing is, you know too much about him, the memory never leaves you.*

One of the men in Jack's barracks knelt at his cot every night, saying a silent prayer. Jack wondered what he said. Was it: *thanks for helping us win the war*...*keeping us safe to fight another day?*

The men out there in the armada heading for Germany were afraid. Today, the fear within them was deeper, more real. Jack was sure of it. But they all did what they had to do, what was deep in every man's soul.

Reaching inside his leather jacket, Jack touched the breast pocket of his flight suit and the newspaper photo of Sarah tucked inside. He remembered her smiling as they walked in New York the summer of 1941, the wind dancing in her hair, picking up the sunlight. The one thought that kept him going throughout the war was the hope that he would see her again one day.

Then he smiled, thinking of Gordon who carried a photo on each mission, not of any one particular girl, just grabbed one from the table by his cot.

The sky looked clear from Jack's cockpit windows. *Now sit back and wait,* he told himself. *Listen to the roar of the engine. It's only a matter of time before the armada reaches the European coast and into the jaws of the Luftwaffe.*

Behind the bomb bay, where the wings intersect the fuselage, gunners Steve, Dave, Earl, Arthur and Joe had unhooked their seat belts and were sitting on the floor. To them it was just another bombing run. Do their job, and hope to hell they make it back.

"Hey Arthur, has anyone asked you what you're going to do when the war is over?" Earl said.

"No," Arthur said, "but I guess I'll do what everyone else will do. Go home, find a nice girl, mom will approve of and raise a family."

"Ohhhh." Dave gave Arthur a friendly punch on the arm. "You're breaking my heart."

"Okay Dave, your turn. Tell these men what you want to do," Steve said. "What you told mom when we were kids."

"You mean go out and save the world?"

"You're kidding. Really?" Earl said. "That's what you're doing now. Think of something more dangerous."

Laughter.

"When this war is over, you know what I'm going to do?" Joe announced, leaning back against the wall of the fuselage.

"Yeah, yeah," Earl knew the answer. "You're going to find Betty Grable and ask her to marry you. We've heard that before, Joe."

Dave shook his head. "We hear that story every day, every mission we climb into this war machine. How many times are we going to tell you, she's already married."

"Yeah to Harry James," Joe said. "I think she likes trumpet players. I'll become one."

"But she's still married," Steve piped in.

Arthur was tired of listening to that old story. "Give it up, Joe." He pulled out a deck of cards from the pocket of his leather jacket—the customary game to bide the time, lighten the oncoming expectation, until they man their respective artillery stations.

Holding the cards, Arthur thrust his hand out. "Who's dealing?"

Chapter 29

Nearing the European coastline tiny black dots hardly visible appeared in the distance, sweeping across the pristine blue sky. It was the German Luftwaffe's Messerschmitt Me262s, single-seat fighter planes flown by the best pilots in the world. The German Me262 "Storm Bird" was faster and more heavily armed than the Allied escorts. Their primary purpose was to annihilate the bombers. The Me262s had been circling the coastline, waiting for the Allied Armada. It was their same pattern. They knew where the armada was coming from and when. But wait, something was terrifyingly different today. As the black dots grew larger, they grew in numbers, stretching deep across the horizon. Thousands and thousands of Me262s emerged. Wave after wave, they just kept coming—a swarm of hornets. There appeared no end.

"Holy shit," Jack said.

"This doesn't look good," Martin said.

Jack shook his head in disbelief. "Only god can help us now."

Shouts fired over the radio from the Mustang and Spitfire pilots as the Me262s headed toward the Allied Armada.

"Here they come."

"Let the music begin."

"Send the Luftwaffe to hell."

"Yeah, we want to go home."

The Allied bomber escorts scrambled, flew ahead to engage the enemy head on, clear the way for the bombers to drop their payload. Live or die, the escorts knew what they had to do—attack the enemy before it had a chance to destroy the bombers, and it was only a matter of seconds before the slow heavy bombers caught up with the escorts.

"Okay men, loosen up," Jack announced, signaling his crew over the B-17 interphone system. "Bogies on the horizon."

The men in the fuselage, playing cards, dumped their hand. It wasn't easy for Arthur—bad timing—he had a royal flush and a two bit bet at stake.

Earl climbed into the top turret while Arthur headed for the tail gun. Steve and Dave helped Joe climb into the ball turret—a Plexiglas sphere attached to the bottom of a B-17, equipped with two guns, and capable of rotating three hundred and sixty degrees. Then Steve sealed the entrance hatch to the ball turret, and he and Dave quickly took position directly opposite each other on each side of the fuselage.

Sliding a door open in the wall of the fuselage, Steve and Dave swiveled their fifty caliber machine gun into position into a frigid sixty degree below zero temperature and a three hundred mile an hour wind. Even wearing three pairs of gloves, frostbite had taken two of Steve's fingers.

Just ahead Mustangs and Spitfires were taking on heavy gun fire, and the bombers were now flying right into the thick of it. Like a packs of wolves, seeking out easy prey, the Me262s headed for the bombers to tear their wings away, ignite eight thousand pounds of bombs, and send them plummeting to earth in a blazing death. All in the hope of saving Nazi ideology.

Every gunner on every B-17 in the sky was firing away to protect their bomb load. Bullets flew everywhere, Mustangs and Spitfires dodged bullets all around. The sky was so crowded, it was impossible to keep from hitting their own. No escort or bomber could escape from being riddled with lead. Amid the constant sound of bullets flying over the radio and the rat-a-tat-tat of the thirteen guns on Fly for Freedom, bombers were exploding right and left, pieces flew away...a wing...a tail narrowly missing Jack's cockpit windows...the side...the front. Mustangs and Spitfires were blown out of the sky one by one. Fighter planes on both sides flew into each other, flew into the bombers, going down in flames, hitting the ground, the impact left a cloud of smoke rising from their grave. It was a flurry of guns pouring death across the sky and it was chaos in its purist form—an unimaginable horror.

A constant flood of screams shot over the radio from terrified men trapped in a fiery coffin—voices of allied escort pilots crying out their last breath of life, flames licking their flesh on the way down...

"Mom, I love you."

"Oh god, help me."

"I love you Mary. Kiss little Billy for me."

"Sorry, mom, your Jimmy boy won't be coming home."

...it went on and on...screaming...screaming...good men dying...too many to count. *What hell—war...what waste...what human cost. Why do men do this? Ego, prove themselves, or something bigger—freedom.* Jack couldn't answer, not even of himself. The smell of death surrounding Jack, sickened him. Even for the strongest of men, it was too much. He dropped his oxygen mask, turned his head down and vomited. Vomited nothing. He gave up having breakfast, could never keep it down.

Tired of hearing the never ending screams, Jack gave Earl an order over the interphone: "Switch off the radio." And when Earl didn't comply fast enough, he shouted, "Switch off the god damn radio!"

*Get control of yourself, Jack...keep flying straight...keep Fly for Freedom steady now...don't let the voices of dying men get to you...you've heard it before...every bombing run. Some of us have to die...that's what war is all about...*he reasoned...*concentrate Jack...important to get to the target...drop the bombs...fulfill the mission...and wish to hell you get your crew back to the base.*

Chapter 30

Exhausted, cold and uncertain of what fate may await him and his crew, Jack turned Fly for Freedom back and headed for home. Reaching the European coastline and the North Sea, he searched the sky for safe escort, a Mustang or Spitfire to guide him back to the base, even though he knew there would probably be none. The base commander had said, coming back, bombers may be on their own.

Jack and his crew had made a successful bomb drop, yet other B-17s were not so blessed. Approaching Berlin, the bombers flew into a wall of smoke created by large amounts of high explosives ejecting from German ground anti-aircraft guns constantly hurling shrapnel—flak—five miles into the sky. The rain of death blew bombers to pieces as one by one they dropped from the sky like bricks. It looked like the bombers had flown into the pit of hell, but this was nothing like hell. Satan himself couldn't even imagine it.

Entering the Berlin airspace, fighter planes from both sides had suddenly disappeared. Allied escort planes couldn't protect the bombers from flak and left the surviving bombers to get to their target and complete the mission on their own. And what the Me262s failed to accomplish, in their attempt to annihilate the surviving bombers, the ground anti-aircraft guns would finish the job.

Fly for Freedom was damaged from shrapnel and riddled with bullet holes in its wings and fuselage, nothing that would prevent Jack from making it safely back to the base. The ground crew could easily perform the repairs overnight, making Fly for Freedom ready for another mission the following day.

Sit back now Jack...he took a deep breath...*listen to the roar of the engine ...having made it back to the coastline, chances are you're home free.*

"We're pretty lucky, Jack, getting in and out," Martin said, relief in his voice. "It was a tough mission. Hitting Germany the way the Allies did today, maybe we're done with this war."

"You mean we could do something with our lives, besides glued to a cockpit seat."

"Three years is a long time," Martin agreed.

Then suddenly as if fate was tempted by what Martin just said, a lone Me262 appeared out of a lone cloud. Martin leaned forward in his co-pilot's seat, squinting through the front cockpit window.

"Bogey two o'clock," Martin announced.

Jack looked to where Martin indicated. A Me262 was cruising steadily in the distance. It didn't appear to be a menace or a threat. *Perhaps a straggler over the North Sea*....Jack assumed...*Or was the German pilot stalking, waiting for the appropriate time to make his move?*

A heavy B-17 bomber was lighter after losing its bomb

load, but still no competition for a single-seat Me262. Jack imagined the enemy pilot wasn't there for a neighborly escort back to a British Airbase. If Jack were the German pilot, he would not let the golden opportunity fly by. The situation was to German pilot's indisputable advantage. The uncertainty made Jack scared, damn scared.

"What's he doing out here?" Martin said as if Jack had the answer.

"He may have friends," Jack said, not eliminating the possibility. In the next breath, he alerted his crew. "Okay, men, we've got company."

The men in the fuselage scrambled, taking their positions at the guns. Earl climbed into the top turret. Arthur went to the tail while Dave and Steve helped Joe climb back into the ball turret, then took their positions again at the sides of Fly for Freedom.

Jack glanced away for a second from the side cockpit window and when he looked back, the Me262 had dropped out of sight.

"Where is he?" Jack said.

Martin searched the sky. "I don't know."

"Anyone see him?" Jack said over the interphone.

All negative responses came from the crew.

The wait seemed forever. Would the Me262 reappear?

"Hey," Arthur called over the interphone. "Someone forgot to tell the Nazis we got the rest of the day off."

"You've got to be joking, right?" Mike said.

"No overtime either. We're not on the clock." Earl

said.

"I'd like to have a piece of mom's apple pie right now." Dave told Steve.

"No time to think about food," his brother said.

"Why not?" Dave said. "If we're going to die, what better thing to think of."

Then suddenly the Me262's thirty millimeter gun was heard coming in fast as it headed for Fly for Freedom's tail.

At the tail gun, Arthur shouted, "I got him lieutenant. He's coming right at me." The sound of the tail gun came loud over the interphone as it competed with the Me262's gun.

What's the German pilot doing? Jack shook his head in disbelief. *Approaching the tail of a B-17 is suicidal.*

Then Arthur's gun fell silent as the Me262's gun continued to hammer away. Through the Me262's gun fire, Arthur's voice came loud and clear over the interphone, "Oh god, my gun's jammed! It's jammed!"

The Me262 soared overhead, its gun still firing away, hitting Earl firing from the fuselage's top turret, evading Bob's gun in the top turret stationed in the cockpit. Then the Me262 turned back, zooming past the tail section from where it came and disappeared.

"Arthur! Arthur!" Jack called over the interphone, but no response.

From the waist gunner's position, Dave reported, "I don't see anything on my side of the fuselage, lieutenant."

"Not from my side either," Steve said. He saw Earl

lying in a pool of blood on the fuselage floor. "Earl got it in the head. I'll go check on Arthur."

"No, stay at your station! We're not clear yet," Jack ordered.

Then the interphone fell silent as the crew waited. Just the constant roar of the engine again to break the silence. Each second seemed to make death more apparent.

Jack searched the sky. Still no sign of the Me262.

"What the hell?" Jack said.

"He's playing with us." Martin fired back.

This lone pilot reminded Jack of the infamous Red Baron, the German ace the colonel went up against in World War I, known to hunt alone, banish the enemy. The British called him the Red Knight.

Nothing you can do, Jack, except keep flying straight. No different than heading to the bombing site through a barrage of Me262s spewing death, except you knew what you were dealing with...this is unknown...intuition tells you the German pilot's not done yet.

Sweat began to trickle down Jack's face. *Wipe it away from your oxygen mask, Jack...if perspiration freezes, it blocks the air flow to your mask.* He wiped away the sweat. *Watch out for head on passes, Jack...the result is an instant kill to the pilot.*

Long wait...

Every surviving gunner gripped their gun tight, watching at their station—Mike and Charlie in the Plexiglas nose in front and just below the cockpit; Steve and Dave at the waist guns; Joe pinned in the belly; and Bob in the top turret behind Jack and Martin in the cockpit.

Suddenly the Me262 reappeared.

"There he is, 12 o'clock," Jack announced over the interphone.

Without hesitation, the Me262 hurled fast toward the nose of Fly for Freedom.

"He's coming in head on!" Charlie shouted. Sitting in the nose, he and Mike could see everything in front of Fly for Freedom.

"Oh my god, he's barreling right at us!" Mike shouted.

The German pilot let loose the Me262's gun firing as it came, weaving side to side to avoid Fly for Freedom's nose guns and the cockpit's top turret gun spewing lead in an attempt to annihilate the Me262, the sound loading the interphone.

Bullets from the Me262's gun broke through and shattered the Plexiglas nose. It pulled up seconds before colliding with Fly for Freedom, swooped over the nose, riddling the cockpit with bullets. As it passed overhead, it made a hard turn right, and avoiding the cockpit's top turret gun, hit Fly for Freedom's fuel tanks under the right wing...did an inverted roll to escape...tipped its wings and peeled off.

In less than four seconds, in a well-executed frontal attack, the German pilot left Fly for Freedom crippled. Smoke poured from its damaged wing.

Jack searched the sky through the side cockpit window in the direction the German pilot disappeared. Tipping his wings was a sign of departure. *Why didn't he finish us off?*

Jack wondered. *Easy target a wounded bomber, throw it into a death spiral, follow the fate of those who went before. Maybe the psychological effect of suffering before death is worse than an immediate death. The German pilot was good, so good, that with all the guns on a B-17, results proved negative. Just like the Red Baron.* Enemy or not, Jack admired his courage.

"He's gone," Jack said. When his co-pilot didn't respond, Jack turned away from the side cockpit window and looked over at Martin. He was slumped over in his seat, blood streaming down his face. Martin didn't know what hit him.

Jack lowered his eyes, reached over and clasped Martin's shoulder. *Perhaps, better a quick death than those plunging to earth, counting the seconds before burning to death.* Now, when Jack needed Martin more than ever to set a damaged B-17 safely on the ground, Jack would have to go it alone.

"All clear men." Jack reported to his crew.

Mike, manning one of the nose guns, had fallen from his seat, facedown on the floor. Plexiglas nose of a B-17 offered no protection against bullets. Charlie stationed next to Mike, rolled him over.

"Hey lieutenant, the Me262 got Mike right in the heart."

"Someone check on Arthur," Jack said.

Dave went to the tail section. "Arthur didn't make it either. Sorry lieutenant."

"Find something to cover them up. Cover them up!" *Take it easy, Jack...nothing you can do for the dead...it won't help the living...pull yourself together...save the rest of your men.*

"We're covering them, lieutenant," Dave said.

"I took care of Mike up here in the nose, lieutenant," Charlie said.

"I'll find something to cover Martin." Bob left his seat behind Jack in the cockpit and headed to the fuselage.

"You okay, lieutenant?" Steve called from the fuselage.

Before Jack could answer, Dave said, "How's it look, lieutenant?" From his waist gunner's position at the right side of the fuselage, he saw the damaged wing. "I mean, she's smoking pretty bad."

"Engine one and two are out." Bob reported.

Jack looked at the right wing through his side cockpit window—it didn't look promising. Only the fuel tanks on the left wing were functional.

"See what you can do about shutting off that fuel in those engines on the right wing." Jack asked his engineer.

"I tried, lieutenant," Bob replied. "Fuel shut off value failed. The fire extinguisher in those engines is not functioning."

Diving would suppress the fire, force the fuel from the wing, but Fly for Freedom was weakened and probably wouldn't withstand the pressure of a steep dive. *She'll have to burn to the ground,* Jack thought.

"I'll be honest with you, men," Jack said. "It'll be a struggle to keep Fly for Freedom airborne, and a rough ride back to base."

"Kind of strange, isn't lieutenant, we made it through the worse part of this mission only to be crippled on the last leg? But we have faith in you," Steve said as if he was attempting to lift the men's spirits, including his own. From a crew's experience, he seemed to know enough about a B-17 that outside of a miracle, the hope of making it to safety seemed unlikely.

"We're with you Lieutenant," Charlie said, "You can land alright. She's tougher than my old lady."

"Okay, all the sweet talk's nice…" Joe said, still in the ball turret, "…but don't you think you should get me out of this sardine tin. If you haven't forgotten, I'm supposed to climb in when the action begins and climb out after, but this is not my permanent residence."

Jack felt a sharp pain in his shoulder and felt wetness against his chest. He reached inside his flight jacket, pulled out his gloved hand saturated with blood. A bullet had pierced his flesh. He didn't feel it at first—just an ache. Stress in the cockpit for long periods of time will sometimes cause muscle aches, possibly confused for a wound…*don't tell the crew, Jack…no need to worry them.*

"Hey lieutenant?" Steve called from the fuselage over the interphone, distress in his voice. "We have a problem here. Can't release Joe from the belly. Track on the ball turret jammed. Hydraulic pump isn't working to rotate the turret. Looks like the gears are damaged. Even the hand crank won't budge to release the hatch." Then he said, "Sorry Joe. I know you can't move, trapped in the belly."

Joe heard the report over the interphone. Crawling into a three foot diameter Plexiglas bubble, lodged tight in a fetal position with twin fifty caliber machine guns pinned against his chest; and a life expectancy in combat of thirty-seven seconds was not Joe's first choice. But he was the smallest crew member, so he volunteered.

"What's the matter with you men?" Joe said. "This has happened before and the ground crew pulled me out. I'll just be walking bent over for a while."

"What will Betty Grable think about that?" Dave joked.

Laughter from the crew came over the interphone. Who better to share laughter with than men who shared a common loyalty?

"Hang in there Joe," Jack said.

"Sure Joe." Steve leaned down over the hatch and gave a couple knocks with his fist on the ball turret.

The pain in Jack's shoulder increased, threatening to interfere with his concentration. He could feel the blood streaming down, drenching the chest of his flight suit. He was tired. The mission was nine hours in and out, and the weight of forty pounds of bulky regalia necessary to keep a pilot warm at high altitudes just added to the fatigue, and with the pain, it was now an internal fight to keep awake.

He looked out the side cockpit window. Fire now licked over the right wing, the smoke heavier. *Doesn't look good.*

There were parachutes in the fuselage, but none of the men were trained in jumping from a B-17. Besides none of the men would leave Joe to save themselves. No other choice but to set Fly for Freedom down. It may not be too late to save the beautiful, magnificent machine that had served Jack well through more than twenty-five missions.

Not far now, Jack.

Jack called to the men over the interphone. "Just a little while now and we can have one last drink before setting our heads down for the night. Turn on the radio, Charlie. We're close enough for the base control tower to pick up our frequency."

Charlie who was trained to fill Earl's position moved from the nose section to Earl's seat and flipped on the radio switch. "Okay, lieutenant, she's got juice."

Jack pressed the microphone closer to his mouth.

"Mayday! Mayday! Mayday! Fly for Freedom calling Horham airbase flight control. I repeat Mayday! Mayday! Mayday!"

Radio static before Jack heard, "This is Horham flight control, we hear you loud and clear Fly for Freedom."

"This is Lieutenant Jack Karsen. Request emergency landing."

"What's your status, lieutenant?"

"Two engines gone, hydraulic system gone." Jack looked at the instrument panel and thc oil gauge. "Losing oil pressure."

"How's your fuel?"

"Critical. Fifteen minutes."

"State your position."

"Heading northwest, ten minutes from base," Jack

said.

"Casualties?"

"Four dead. Gunner trapped in belly."

"Stand by."

Long wait...

Every second counted….

Be patient, Jack…you know what patience is…it takes over an hour to get a B-17 to twenty-five thousand feet, climbing only three hundred feet per minute, not to mention getting all those B-17s in stacked formation…your thoughts are rambling…pay attention, Jack…it's the pain sharper than before.

"Fly for Freedom, this is Horham flight control. Proceed to runway."

Jack made a wide turn for the approach. Through the side cockpit window and into view, B-17s were landing one after another coming back from the bombing run.

Only a little longer…just a little longer…feeling drowsy.

"Fly for Freedom, this is Horham flight control, B-17 landing ahead of you. Stand by."

"Did he say land or standby…he said standby…no he already said standby…yes, he said to land…you're nodding off, Jack…stay awake…only a few more minutes…you can do it…no, no, you're nodding off…..

"Fly for Freedom, this is Horham flight control, you are clear to land."

With no response from Jack, the control tower repeated the instructions.

"Fly for Freedom, you are clear to land."

Still no answer.

'Fly for Freedom, this is Horham flight control, please respond."

Jack jerked awake, rubbed his eyes and face to help him stay awake. He no longer needed his oxygen mask below ten thousand feet, now dangling by a strap from his leather cap.

"Fly for Freedom, we need you to respond."

"Affirmative," Jack said.

"Good luck lieutenant."

Okay Jack…get this baby down. Remember, she may be easy to set down without damage, but try landing a crippled plane that's as tall as a two story building with a wingspan four times that much…your thoughts are drifting, Jack…stay on course.

The B-17 attempting to land ahead was in bad shape, no tail and a hole ripped in the fuselage. If it didn't clear the runway, Jack would have to land on it, and both planes would parish. Panic rose in Jack. He tightened his grip on the cockpit wheel.

Just ahead the B-17 slammed down hard on the runway, skidded into the field, but cleared the runway.

*Okay Jack, you're clear…you can set Fly for Freedom down…you've done it many times…descend to one thousand feet, standard visual approach for landing…drop three hundred feet per minute… there it is, right in front of you, a beautiful strip of concrete…only a little longer Jack…hold on…*he told himself…*now line up…okay…you're doing good, you'll be on the ground in three minutes…pull back slowly on the throttle to reduce speed…slowly…slowly….*

Smoke from the right wing rose intermittently across

the front cockpit window, obstructing his view.

I can't see the runway...where's the runway? Doesn't matter Jack, you're lined up.

The pain dug deeper now, the desire to sleep, heavier. He shivered. Cold. *Got to fight the cold, Jack. Result could be shock. No, no, you're nodding off again. Wake up Jack!* He rubbed his eyes again. *Okay now descending...descending....* He needed god's hands on the cockpit wheel now more than ever.

"Come on baby...come on baby," Joe called to the B-17 and Jack could hear his voice over the interphone, "you can make it baby, you can make it," Joe said.

*Oh no, it's stalling...don't stall...don't stall on me...*we've *almost there...lower the wing flaps that should help the stalling...but remember the pilot's manual, Jack...don't lower the flaps in excess of one hundred forty miles per hour.* Why was he thinking this? Second nature to a pilot like putting on your shoes every morning.

Okay, Jack, the flaps are down...reduce speed to 120mph...steady...steady ...now the landing gear...time to drop the landing gear...the landing gear, Jack...remember.

He looked over at the control panel to find the toggle switch for the landing gear. When he reached for it, the pain in his shoulder sharpened, and forced him to pull back. *You've got to get this plane on the ground...try again, Jack.* He reached for the switch again, pushing against the pain. The switch wouldn't budge—jammed. If Jack didn't free the switch, the belly gunner would be crushed on landing. He tried again...again. "Come on, come on," Jack said desperation in his voice. Each attempt produced no results. Suddenly the green light indicator on the switch flickered rapidly then went dead. *Oh god, no.*

In Joe's line of sight no wheels dropped on approach.

"Hey, lieutenant," Joe called over the interphone. "I don't see the wheels. Did you forget?" Why did Joe ask that? Jack wouldn't have forgotten.

No response from Jack.

"Lieutenant…lieutenant…."

There was still no response from Jack.

Suddenly Joe feared the worse.

"Steve, get on the landing gear's hand crank," Jack ordered, and Steve jumped up.

It appeared Steve had to work fast. Something went wrong with the landing gear switch, or the use of the hand crank wasn't necessary. He worked feverishly in an attempt to get the crank to do its job. One wheel lowered halfway, the other not at all.

"Let me try." Dave pushed Steve out of the way. Every second counted, but his attempts to turn the crank failed. "No good, lieutenant. Frozen."

There was silence on the interphone.

Then Jack was about to say one of the hardest things he ever said in his life, and wish to god he didn't have to say it. He swallowed hard. "Sorry Joe, it doesn't look good."

Jack didn't have to say anything. Joe had listened over the interphone, the exchange between Steve, Dave and Jack. Without landing wheels, the ball turret would never withstand the pressure of a forty thousand pound B-17 slamming down on the runway. He had heard similar stories about men getting stuck in the ball turret, and when the B-17 landed on its belly, the ground crew had to wash the man out with a hose. Nothing more could be done for Joe. Eminent death becomes more profound when it is certain.

Then in a quiet voice, Joe said, "It's alright, lieutenant. I heard it over the interphone." Then there was a long pause as if Joe was gathering courage he never thought he had. "We gave Hitler a good run, didn't we? Kiss the ground when you get back home. And hey, I'm proud to have known you men." Then there was a mumbling sound over the interphone—Joe was praying.

Tears welled up in Jack's eyes. *That's what kind of men are in this hell called war.*

Through no fault of their own, Steve and Dave felt powerless. They sat in the fuselage, now strapped in their seatbelts. The horror of the scene about to unfold ran through their minds. They didn't look at each other or say a word. What could be said?

Suddenly fire ignited in the cabin. No time to put it out, the remaining crew were secured in their seatbelts, bracing for a hard landing. Only a matter of seconds left before the plane hit the runway with full force.

Dropping fast now…

A song broke out in the fuselage. Steve began singing…

...O beautiful for spacious skies,
For amber waves of grain,
For purple mountains majesties,
Above the fruited plain!...

...then Joe in the belly, tears in his eyes, joined in, followed by the remaining crew, coming loud and clear over the interphone...

...America! America!
God shed His grace on thee,
And crown thy good with brotherhood,
From sea to shining—

—sirens blared as ambulance trucks raced toward the grassy expanse along the runway of Horham aifield where flames rose high. Fly for Freedom which had served Jack well through the war and the war machine Charlie had said was tougher than his old lady, was steel melting in an open field.

Chapter 31

"Where is he?"

"Bed seven," the nurse told the doctor.

The doctor walked down the ward of the military hospital in Malvern England, past the beds lined on each side where every bed was occupied with war wounded. So many trying to heal before going home. Only half the injured coming into the ward survived. Men left with missing limbs, paralyzed or blinded for life from shrapnel, most psychologically traumatized. Few escaped unscathed by the ravages of war.

Reaching bed seven, the doctor lifted a clip board hanging at the foot of the bed, and flipped through the pages of notes on the medical chart. He replaced it then walked around to the side of the bed.

"You were lucky Lieutenant Karsen to come out of that crash with only a broken leg. Oh, you were pretty banged up with bruises, but those heal quickly so will the bullet wound in your shoulder."

From where he lay flat on the bed, Jack pulled himself up by the bar hanging across his bed, his broken leg in a sling. He grabbed the doctor by his white coat, pulled the doctor close to him. "Hey doctor, what about my crew?"

The nurse attending a soldier in the next bed, noticed Jack's reaction, and came immediately to the aid of the doctor.

"Can I help doctor?" she said.

The doctor pulled Jack's hand away from his grip, and Jack fell back on the bed. Jack's reaction didn't seem to bother the doctor he was obviously used to it. He had the experience of two wars. He was an ambulance driver during World War I before taking the Hippocratic Oath. Soldiers came into the military hospital with experiences he evidently could only imagine. War does terrible things to a man.

Jack said, "No one wants to tell me anything, say I have to wait for you."

The doctor hesitated, glanced at the nurse standing next to him then looked back at Jack. Another soldier he had to tell bad news.

"We kept you heavily sedated. We do that to most soldiers who suffer from traumatic shock. You were thrown from the plane before it exploded. I'm sorry lieutenant, you were the only survivor."

Tears came to Jack's eyes. He turned his face away, the sorrow was too profound. They went through training together…laughed…told each other their deepest thoughts. He visualized the cots folded over.

"You couldn't save them lieutenant. Their mortality lies in the memory of their sacrifice." He touched Jack's arm in a sign of comfort. "They have given you a gift, lieutenant. You live your life for all of them. Make it worthwhile."

The doctor started to leave, but turned back. "By the

way," he said as he reached into the pocket of his white coat and pulled out the folded news clipping. "This was in your flight suit. Looks like something you wanted very much to keep." He laid it on the table next to Jack's bed and walked away.

Chapter 32

Jack sat on a bench in the quiet solitude of the park adjoining the military hospital. The lush lawn stretching long before him was dotted with benches filled with recovering military. He listened to a bird singing without a care on a tree branch above him as a yellow butterfly fluttered from one flower to the next, finding its way through the colors clustered along the walkway. It was a peace he had not known since before he had entered the war. Combat stress and seeing tremendous loss of human life, horrors no man should witness, changed him. War makes a young man mature quickly.

A nurse appeared at his side, interrupting his feeling of gratitude for the surrounding serenity.

"Would you like to write a letter?" she said.

"A letter?" Jack said with no emotion.

"Yes. Maybe I can write it for you," the nurse said.

Jack was perfectly capable of doing so himself, but the hospital staff was encouraged to accommodate the soldiers whenever possible. He knew he had to give an answer, but to whom would he write a letter? His father had died before Jack left for Britain, and his brother who was helping his mom run the farm, was drafted after the Japanese bombed Pearl Harbor. With both her sons in the war, the worry of either of them ever coming home drove his mother to any early grave.

His brother was an Army Private in the 29th Infantry Division. Jack didn't know where he was in the war until the invasion of Normandy and the report that the 29th Infantry Division was in the first wave to hit the beach at Omaha, June 6, 1944, the morning after Jack's fateful mission. Almost no one survived the first wave—the sea turned red.

If he could write to Sarah, his tormented heart would be eased, but his unanswered letter, would be worse than not writing at all. All he could think of was getting away from this god forsaken war. Right now, he just wanted to go back to the farm.

"Lieutenant?" the nurse said.

With no answer, and Jack still staring in the distance, the nurse proceeded to set the pencil and paper beside him on the bench.

"Perhaps I can leave the paper here…" she suggested "…you can compose it and I'll post it for you."

The nurse quietly turned to leave, walking down the path from where she came. As she walked toward the brick hospital building seen in the short distance, she passed Gordon who was on his way to visit Jack. As she passed, Gordon turned to give her the *once over*—looking her up and down—then smiled. Sweet young chic in his mind. Why didn't she turn and take notice, a handsome guy like him, dressed in his khakis. He wanted to whistle, but considering where he was, it wouldn't have been appropriate. He turned back to make his way toward Jack still sitting on the bench.

Noticing Gordon walking toward him, Jack rose from his seat to greet his visitor. Seeing Gordon lessened this sense of loneliness and his face formed a well needed smile. He grabbed his cane hanging over the arm of the bench and braced his weight heavily upon it.

"Gordon."

"Yeah, buddy, it's me."

Jack hobbled a few steps toward Gordon.

"Hey, take it easy," Gordon said when he saw Jack weak on his feet. "You don't have to get up for me. Save it for the ladies."

Jack laughed. *Same old Gordon.* Jack sat back on the bench. Gordon sat beside him. Removing his hat, Gordon set it down on the space between them, concealing the pad and pencil, the nurse left.

"I heard you got through alright," Jack said.

"Never made my drop. Trouble with one of the engines. Had to turn back." Then Gordon said sadly, "Sorry about your crew."

Then Joe's words flashed across Jack's mind: *Kiss the ground when you get back home.* Jack couldn't help thinking why was he spared? *It's not your time yet Jack,* he told himself.

"You mustn't blame yourself. It's war," Gordon said. "Every time they got into that B-17, they all told themselves it was the last time. Hell, we all did."

Then Jack remembered what the doctor had said: *They have given you a gift. You live your life for all of them.* Jack smiled slightly, appreciative of Gordon's concern. "I'm glad you're here Gordon. Not just that you're here, but you made it."

"Yeah."

"Overall, how'd we do that day?" Jack said.

"Losses were extreme. I don't know the final count of B-17s and Allied escorts lost." Gordon was silent for a moment in reverence, then he said, "But here's the good news, you probably already know, read it in the newspaper. The following day after our bombing run, one hundred fifty-six thousand men landed on the beaches at Normandy. That's why we scaled up the bombing the day before, to lead the way for the land invasion. It was the largest invasion ever assembled. Codename *Operation Overlord.* Pretty much caught the Germans by surprise. The German Panzer Division was stationed at Calais, believing the Allied forces would land at the shortest route from the English coast across the Channel to France. Allied forces had been planning the operation for months. It won't be long before our troops march straight into Berlin, and the war in Europe will be over. Then the focus is definitely on the Pacific."

"Are you going to sign up for a Pacific tour?" Jack had contemplated the possibility.

"Hell no," He obviously didn't consider himself as brave as Jack. "I hope you're not thinking of it. Leave it to the younger men coming in fresh. War is grueling. The body can only take so much stress and seeing the constant pool of death everyday plays havoc on the psyche. We've been lucky so far, but I'm not about to tempt fate any longer."

What Gordon said made sense, but it had always been in Jack's character to not give up when the job wasn't done.

"So, I hear you're being discharged," Gordon said on a happier note. "Hey, what do say, we get the hell out of this joint, and go back to the states?"

"What do you want to do?" Jack said.

"We'll figure it out."

1948

Chapter 33

On her death bed moments before her last breath, Charlotte offered Sarah advice. Words she regretted not saying long ago.

Early one evening in the family dining room of the Wescott mansion, Charlotte complained of a stomach ailment and excused herself to retire. Later that evening, she became overcome by a raging fever, shivering intermittently with chills.

The following morning, Charlotte's condition grew worse, and the family doctor was called to the residence where he assured the family members that it was a simple infection, left antibiotics and administered instructions. But three days later, the infection had spread to her blood stream, and there was nothing that could be done for blood poisoning. "Sepsis," the doctor diagnosed and said it was not uncommon for doctors to recognize it too late. Her system appeared unable to fight it.

The doctor informed family members that it was only a matter of hours before she passed, and he suggested they say their goodbyes, one by one.

Winston appeared so overwrought, that it was apparent he found difficulty saying goodbye to the woman who had been by his side for more years than he cared to count. Without saying a word, he motioned with a nod of his head that Sarah should go into Charlotte's room first.

Sarah entered Charlotte's bedroom and walked slowly to Charlotte's bedside, where she lay quietly in a high poster bed. The sound of her heavy breathing filled the room with the feeling of oncoming death. The dim light from a lonely lamp on the nightstand cast ominous shadows across the wall.

Charlotte opened her eyes when she sensed a presence at her bedside..

"Sarah, dear, I know the worse. The doctor told me."

"Oh, mother." Sarah cried and knelt at Charlotte's bedside, burying her head in her mother's lap.

Charlotte placed her hand on Sarah's head, patting it gently. "Now we have no time for that," she said, and Sarah lifted her head, tears staining her face. Charlotte had difficulty breathing so she wanted to say what she felt needed to be said with as few words as possible.

Rising to her feet, Sarah dried her tears.

"Sarah, I know you have not been happy with George." Charlotte's weak voice began. "Sarah, my darling, your life is comfortable as was mine. We were very lucky that way, and you have two lovely children, that in itself is fulfilling. But I have seen in your eyes over the years what has been in mine. The truth behind the lack of happiness is there."

Charlotte turned inward and looked at her life. It wasn't until now that she was given the luxury of examining it and calling it for what it truly was, and she was saying words she would not have said otherwise. It made no difference now for she was free to think and say as she wished in her last breath of life.

Charlotte said, “I had seen a glow in your face when you once spoke of your soldier. You should have been with him. A mother knows her daughter’s heart better than anyone. Times are changing, Sarah. Find what makes you happy. Find it, hold onto it. Fill the empty part of your heart.”

Sarah appeared surprised. In that moment she could feel the truth in her mother’s words that someday, somehow, she must be with Jack.

“Mother, why didn’t you tell me this before?”

“I thought you’d forget, but I was wrong. We all have things we have to live with.” Her eyes grew distant as if she was reliving something in her past she had kept secret. Then she closed her eyes tight, as if releasing the past she could not change. A tear rolled down her cheek. She opened her eyes and gazed at Sarah. She had always wished for more children, but felt blessed to have the companionship of one precious life.

“Don’t be too hard on your father, Sarah. He does what he feels is right for everyone.”

The door opened and the doctor appeared.

“It’s time for your father to come in,” he said, quietly.

“Oh mother, I can’t go.” She knelt by Charlotte’s bedside again, weeping.

“Be brave Sarah. We must all be brave.”

“I can’t.”

"You must try."

Sarah rose and dried her tears. "Yes mother, I'll try."

When Sarah started to leave, Charlotte reached for Sarah's hand with one last request. "Your father...you're all he's has now."

Sarah kissed her mother on the forehead, and Charlotte reached for Sarah's hand again.

"I love you, Sarah," Charlotte whispered.

As Sarah left the room, wiping her tears, she passed her father in the hall. Not a word was exchanged between them as he entered Charlotte's room.

Louise had passed. George's mother and father had followed. All that was left of the past generation was Winston, and with him an obligation imposed on Sarah to fulfill the indirect request from the lips of a dying woman.

***

After Charlotte's death, Winston became more and more despondent as time went by. He had come to rely on Charlotte more than anyone had imagined. Now it was Sarah he turned to and she did what she could to fill her mother's place, but it proved unsuccessful. Consumed with grief, he lost his will to live. Hard to believe that a man so obsessed with maintaining his social status in the community, ruling his financial and family life with an iron fist for the sake of the Westcott name, would just give up. But it appeared he realized he had lost the woman to whom he had shown so very little affection, and perhaps now regretted it. Loneliness can destroy the will to live.

Two years after Charlotte passed away Winston retired one night and died peacefully in his sleep. At least he was granted that comfort.

1951

Chapter 34

The war had been over for six years. Sarah had often thought of Martha whether her hopes and dreams were fulfilled. When Sarah had inquired at the Red Cross, she was told Martha's soldier didn't come home.

Sarah wondered if Jack came home or if he was even alive. She never checked further since her trip to the U.S. War Department in 1943, and when hope of ever having a life with Jack seemed forever lost, something always appeared to drag her back—first her mother's words on her deathbed, and now, the article in the day's national newspaper.

George returned home from his office to have the butler inform him, "Madam has gone to a late tea. She is expected to return within the hour."

"Thank you, Harrington." George handed the butler his hat, and the butler disappeared into another room off the central hall.

George went into the library and to a table of crystal decanters holding various spirits. He poured a shot of whiskey into a crystal glass and downed the contents in one swallow.

He felt more confident than ever. Prosperity America witnessed during the war had continued as the economy grew ever stronger. The demand for steel had made the

Wescott and Minton business enterprises wealthy beyond measure, and with it, George. He was falling meticulously into Winston's mold, and he was truly Winston's son more than he was his own father's son.

He refilled the glass with a generous amount of whiskey and set it down long enough to grab a cigar from a silver box near the decanters. He took the cigar and the glass with him to the other side of the room and settled down in chair to relax.

When he turned to set the glass on the table beside him in order to light the cigar, he noticed the daily newspaper lying on the table. It was folded in such a way to reveal an article with a photo that appeared to be of particular interest. He picked up the paper and began to read…

…Jack Karsen noted New York architect honored at a Mayoral event and presented with the prestigious Architect of the Year Award. The award is just one of the many Karsen has received honoring gifted architects throughout the U.S.

Karsen, a World War II veteran fought for Britain, and then the U.S. when America entered the war. Karsen shares his great success by giving generously to many local and national charities. Karsen and his partner Gordon Frazer are located in the Karsen, Frazer building in New York…

…*Hmm…* George thought, *Karsen,..interesting man.*

Curiosity drew him to look closer at the photo, staring intensely at it. He never met the man, but there was something vaguely familiar about him. Karsen appeared to bear a striking resemblance to Philip, but George dismissed the thought as quickly as it came, blaming it on an unnecessary suspicion. *Just an article Sarah may have looked at, and unknowingly folded it that way and left it.*

Still, the thought continued to irritate him as he fingered the edge of the newspaper page. Since Sarah came home from her trip to New York, two weeks before their marriage, her innermost thoughts seemed lost. Something caused a change between them.

Was he worrying unnecessarily? She was a dutiful wife. He was satisfied so why should he come to an irrational conclusion, fanaticize over some newspaper article? Besides Sarah would never put shame on the family, and he would never confront her, accuse her of something of which he had no proof. He couldn't do that to Sarah, he loved her too much and like a Wescott, a Minton had an overabundance of pride.

Chapter 35

It was a chilly fall morning when Jack left an office building in Boston's central business district and walked out onto Water Street. He had just secured a contract to design a sixty story modern office and retail building for a prominent law firm. Designing buildings in major cities on the east coast was not new to him, but it was the first in Boston.

He had never been to *The Cradle of Liberty* Boston's nickname, and his first thought when he received the call that his design was accepted—was of Sarah. Now he felt closer to her just breathing the Boston air and the thought blossomed in his mind of what life would have been like if she came to the train that summer night in 1941. The true reason she didn't appear never ceased to haunt him, and memories grew sharper walking in the footsteps she may have walked.

He declined an offer from his clients to have lunch at the Union Oyster House, the oldest restaurant in Boston which had opened in 1826. Boston was considered one of the most walkable cities in the U.S. so why not stretch his legs, and familiarize himself with Boston. Walking always cleared his head after an intense meeting and reminded him of the many steps he walked across the cornfield. Perhaps he might find a hotdog stand along the way, but he doubted it would compare to one in New York.

Sheltering against the wind, he buttoned his trench coat, his feet shuffling through the autumn leaves scattered heavy along the street. He passed historic structures where gas lit streets and brick sidewalks were commonplace in old Boston. On Washington Street, he glanced up at the Winthrop Building, first steel frame skyscraper in Boston, and paused to admire Old City Hall, an extraordinary example of the French Second Empire Period. And then he found himself in Beacon Hill, a residential area for Boston's Upper-Class since the colonial days. Finding an empty park bench in Boston Common near the corner of Park and Tremont Streets, he decided to rest and enjoy the solitude. The park appeared empty, except for a couple sitting on a bench across the park, chatting, their distant voices lifting with the wind.

Boston Common was the oldest historic park in the country, home of puritanical punishments of whipping posts, stocks and pillory, including witches hung from the tree now long gone known as the Great Elm. British soldiers once rested in the park after the taking of Bunker Hill. Boston history seemed of particular interest to him, because of Sarah.

The couple sitting on the bench left, walking toward Beacon Street then disappeared. It was peaceful. No one to share the park. There was just the sound of the wind rustling the leaves on the trees, and the clinking of the chains hanging from the seats of a lonely swing set, swaying in the strength of the wind.

In the quiet solitude a woman and two children emerged from one of the mansions of stately elegance, lining Beacon Street across the park. It was a three story brick and white granite exterior with an ornate carving above the front entry. Balconies were laced with iron railings and an iron fence surrounded the property. It was quite impressive to his architectural eye, a prime example of Georgian architecture. It would have once been a palace to him as a young man walking out of a cornfield.

Taking the children's hands, the woman walked down the stone steps, through the tall iron gate and crossed the street to the park. The boy appeared about nine years old and the girl, seven. They were wearing coats. The boy wore a pea coat and a mariner's cap. A headscarf covered the woman's head, tied in a knot under her chin, small fragments of auburn finding their way about her face. They headed toward the swings, where each child took a seat.

Jack could hear their voices in the distance, but couldn't make out what was said, except they sounded happy. As he watched them from afar, he suddenly became mesmerized by the woman's image. Then he realized the woman was Sarah. *Sarah. Undeniably Sarah.*

Of all the past moments in life, how could this one possibly bring them together? In his longing so many times, he wanted to locate her, call her, but it wasn't right to interfere in her life, and for him, it would bleed open a long enduring wound.

Then he wondered about the children that they must be hers. He pulled the collar of his trench coat up in an attempt to conceal his identity, but he was at a safe distance that he was almost certain, she wouldn't look his way. But if she did, he would get up from the bench and walk away.

Jack continued to watch them as the wind grew stronger, hurling leaves in all directions. Suddenly, a gust of wind came up and whipped the boy's cap from his head, blowing it twirling across the park in Jack's direction. Jumping from his swing, the boy ran after it as the wind carried it further away.

Suddenly the cap landed at Jack's feet. Jack bent down to pick it up and when he rose, the boy was standing in front of him, eye to eye. For a moment, looking into the boy's face, Jack was stunned. There was something mysteriously familiar about him.

"Sorry sir, that's my cap," the boy said.

Without saying a word, Jack handed the boy his cap.

"Thank you, sir," the boy said, grabbing his cap from Jack's hand. And as quickly as the boy had appeared, he raced away, back from his adventure, to cross the park from where he came.

Sarah looked up from where she had been tying Mary's shoe, and saw Philip running toward her.

"Where did you go Philip?"

"The wind blew my hat off and this man sitting on the bench over there…" he said as he pointed across the park, "…picked it up for me."

Sarah looked to where Philip had pointed, but all she saw was a lonely bench.

"What did he look like?"

"I don't know," he shrugged. "Just a man."

1964

Chapter 36

A few blocks from his office, Jack instructed his driver to pull over.

"Stop here. I'll walk."

The driver pulled up to the curb on New York's Park Avenue.

As Jack opened the backdoor of the Rolls-Royce, he said, "Take my briefcase to the office."

Jack left the car, crossed the street and headed down Park Avenue. He loosened his tie, and unbuttoned the collar of his dress shirt. He was done for the day, time to relax.

He walked to an art gallery he was familiar with, having made several purchases in the past. The gallery owner was on the phone when Jack entered so Jack browsed through the gallery.

A few years ago, Jack could only imagine success he now knew. He and Gordon had come so far in such a short time. Gordon had said the success was owed to Jack, his talent as an architect, talent that can't be taught, but since Gordon handled the financial aspect, investing and expanding the business, he in Jack's judgment, was the true mastermind.

Business was doing so well that he and Gordon had expanded their firm to six floors of the Karsen, Frazer building, increasing the size of Jack's personal office. A view of art gracing the walls of his new office would not only be pleasant for him, but suitable to give the impression of success to his clients. Clients want to retain a professional with an eye for beauty in all forms of design. He didn't know quite what he was looking for, but he would know it when he saw it.

As he walked slowly along the gallery, he paused only briefly at each work of art, until he noticed a fairly large oil painting where the subject appeared familiar to him—an old wooden house almost hidden by a vast field of corn under a blazing blue sky. He could almost feel the warmth of the sun shining on the rows of cornstalks, and hear the sound of their long leaves whispering in the wind. "I would love to see Iowa someday," he remembered Sarah saying.

Suddenly it became clear. As he looked for the artist name on the lower right hand corner of the painting, the gallery owner who had hung up the phone, cheerfully approached Jack.

Jack was one of his best customers, having made purchases in his gallery and at auction of paintings of some of the great masters.

"Mr. Karsen, how can I help you?"

Jack didn't answer, lost in the past.

"Have you heard of Sarah Wescott Minton?" the gallery owner said, noticing Jack admiring the painting of the cornfield. "You know her as an artist?"

"When did she start painting?" Jack said.

"1962, I believe. She went to art school in Boston. Many great painters started later in life...Cezanne, Monet, Gauguin, Van Gogh." he said their names as if singing them "Her landscapes are unique and have a rare quality you find among the world's greatest artists. She has an innate ability to work in all mediums. Apparently from what I understand, she's never been to a cornfield." Admiringly the gallery owner gazed at Sarah's work.

"Extraordinary, don't you think?" the gallery owner said. "Notice the way she captures the light. Rows and rows of cornstalks, and the wooden house dwarfed by their magnitude—the depth, the clarity. Makes you feel you are experiencing what she sees. She calls it: *god's poetry.*"

Jack smiled. It was exactly as he had described his farm the day they met. He wondered if her eyes were still as blue as the sky in the painting.

"When was it painted?" Jack said.

"Completed this year."

"This year?"

"First time in our gallery." the gallery owner said. "Her paintings are becoming quite well known, and sought after. All her work is original. She never duplicates a work. We were lucky to be able to display two."

"Two?"

"Yes, the watercolor abstract next to it. Both came in this morning."

The gallery owner stepped aside so Jack could view it.

"Notice..." the gallery owner began to describe the

second painting of equal size, "...the soldier sitting on the bench alongside the girl both colored in gray with no variation of any other color, their faces indiscernible, but denoting a sense of loneliness, as if they were saying goodbye. Note, the subtle blend of colors in the overall work, the shades of green and gray, the touch of pink on the edge of the clouds, the blue sky across the park. Captures the emotions of the moment. You can almost feel her strokes glide across the canvas. Perfect."

"Yes, perfect in every way." Jack glanced at the right hand corner of the painting and its title: *Summer 1941*. The painting said everything he needed to know. Someday, he believed, he would know why she vanished from his life.

"I'll take it," Jack said.

"Which one?"

"Both."

The gallery owner appeared delighted. Although Jack never asked the price of any art he purchased from the gallery, the gallery owner looked as though he was obligated to inform him.

"They are very expensive, Mr. Karsen," the gallery owner said, accentuating the word *very*.

Jack gave the gallery owner a look to express that price was not a consideration. Love of art doesn't have a price.

"Deliver to your Fifth Avenue address, Mr. Karsen?"

"To my office." Jack spent more time in the office than his eight thousand square foot Fifth Avenue apartment overlooking Central Park.

"Deliver them tomorrow." Jack handed the gallery owner his business card with his office address, then said, "I am to remain anonymous."

Chapter 37

"You will have the electrical work completed by this evening." Jack told the electrician who was installing spotlights. "Two paintings will be delivered tomorrow, and hung on these walls. Once they arrive, the gallery owner will adjust the spotlights in the right position to enhance the colors."

"Yes, Mr. Karsen, I understand."

Gordon appeared, poked his head inside Jack's office.

"What's going on in here, Jack?"

Jack pulled Gordon into the hall outside his office and closed the door. "I found the perfect art for my office." Jack had always imagined seeing Sarah on every street corner, the other side of an opened door, but now he can see her every day. If he could never touch her again, he would never stop loving her. He gave himself to her that night in 1941 when he said: "I want you to hold onto my heart and never let go."

"You never went through this much trouble before," Gordon said.

"This is different."

"Really? This I have to see."

Chapter 38

It was at the New York's LaGuardia Airport when Jack walked back into Sarah's life.

Sarah had stopped at the airport convenience store to pick up something to read on her return to Boston after her annual New York shopping trip. This year's June shopping trip was postponed until fall. Philip and Mary wanted to spend the entire summer during their school break at the Wescott summer home on Cape Cod. And Sarah's greatest pleasure in life was to be with them. They had brought friends, and it was so wonderful to have youthful, happy voices surrounding her.

Sarah went directly to the magazine rack on the side of the store, and began flipping through various periodicals to find one of interest. She was still youthful looking with the same petite figure she had as a young girl. And she never lost the poise and air of dignity of a Westcott woman who was expected to make regular trips to a salon, and maintain a wardrobe of the latest fashions, especially when her husband entertained the most respectable people in business and Boston society.

She was still standing at the magazine rack when Jack walked into the store. He had just landed from Philadelphia, and thought he would pick up a newspaper to read on the ride back to his office.

Jack headed for the newspapers stacked on a stand by the cashier's counter at the front of the store. He set his briefcase on the floor then grabbed the New York Times. As he looked up toward the cashier, he thought he noticed Sarah on the side of the store, partially hidden by a rack of books. On closer look, it was Sarah, he was certain. In all the airports, in all the cities, there she was, kindling his heart to live again.

The cashier, a man in his twenties, noticed Jack's attention was drawn to another part of the store and the cashier appeared as if he was wondering if Jack wanted to do business, because Jack was holding up his time. "Do you want the newspaper?" the cashier said.

Jack paid the cashier with a hundred dollar bill.

"Keep the change," Jack said, and the cashier looked surprised. No one had ever done that before.

Then Jack said, "Do you see the woman by the magazine rack?"

The cashier looked toward the rack, saw the woman Jack was referring to then turned back to Jack.

"Yes," the cashier said.

Jack flipped out his business card from his inside pocket. "Give her my card. I'll be in the coffee shop." He picked up his briefcase and left.

Not finding anything of interest, Sarah made her way to the convenience store entrance to leave when the cashier called to her:

"Miss?"

She turned back and approached the cashier's counter,

wondering what the cashier wanted. The cashier handed her Jack's card.

She looked at the card—*Jack*. He came back from the war that much she knew through the news article about his success as an architect. She had often wondered what life would have been for them if she had waited for him, and whether his heart was as heavy as hers, yearning for what seemed the impossible.

"He's in the coffee shop…" the cashier said, "…nice man."

As she walked toward the coffee shop, every moment of that day in New York flowed back to her as if it was just yesterday, and she smiled sweetly.

Jack. Jack. Thoughts ran through her mind in no particular order. How did he recognize her? How would she act? What would she say? She didn't have time to prepare. She had thought she would never see him again, and even if he would remember her the way she had him all those years.

She stopped frozen outside the coffee shop. *I shouldn't go. I can't go.* Then she thought, *How silly, you're acting like a school girl. Nothing can come from it, so what harm can it do? It's just a meeting of old friends*…she convinced herself and entered the coffee shop.

The room was filled with the usual sounds of travelers' voices, bustling waitresses, clinking of dishes, and the sweet and pungent smells coming from the kitchen. Standing at the entrance, she searched the many faces sitting at tables and in booths...until…suddenly…her eyes fell upon him.

From a quiet booth in the back of the coffee shop, Jack rose from his seat in a gesture to greet her when he saw her approach, a smile forming on his face.

He changed but little. Just as slender as he was when they first met. Except for greying at the temples of his thick, raven hair, he was the same Jack, skin just as smooth, but for a few wrinkles around the eyes.

Immediately she noticed his European dark blue, silk suit, matching vest, white silk shirt, and red tie—surely the sign of success—dressed handsomely and in good taste. He no longer appeared that young man in the dark blue military uniform going off to war, twenty-three years ago, the only way she had to remember him. But then, she wasn't the same. Now, she was forty-three and he was forty-five. The war and life had changed both of them. There were so many things she had wanted to say if she ever saw him again, but now all she could think of was her heart pounding so loud surely he could hear it.

She waited for him to speak.

"Hello Sarah."

"Jack."

At last, there was her voice he had longed to hear, those blue eyes forever in his mind, and her perfume, the sweet scent of fresh cut flowers brought in from the fields—memories of their night together, heightening his desire for her. He dreamed of this moment and if it would ever be. He wanted to take her in his arms, kiss every inch of her body.

"I'm so surprised, Jack." She sat across from him, unbuttoning the collar of her coat, but didn't remove it. Could this possibly mean to Jack her visit wouldn't be long?

"Nice surprise, I hope."

"Yes, it is," she said. "I often wondered about you through the years and hoped you were safe in the war and would come home."

The war. He didn't want to think about the war, never talked about it. Even he and Gordon never spoke of it again. The memories of his lost crew were still deep in his mind. Men, he and Gordon knew too well. Men who would give their life for each other.

"I prayed a lot." Jack gave Sarah the simple answer, but true.

"So you didn't go to the Pacific after the war in Europe?"

"No, the war was over for me after the invasion at Normandy."

"Do you miss flying?"

He had no answer. Best left unremembered.

The waitress appeared. "What would you like?"

"Two coffees. Black and one with cream." He noticed the way Sarah looked at him. He remembered.

The waitress nodded then walked away.

There was the diamond on the ring finger of her left hand. It didn't mean anything to him anymore than it did in 1941. Staring closely at the jewel, he felt the urge to ask:

"Do you love him?"

She appeared startled at his question, but then she answered honestly. "He's the father of my children."

With the mention of her children, the memory of that day in Boston came to him, where the wind blew the boy's cap across the park to land at his feet.

"How about you Jack?"

"Never married."

The waitress brought the coffee, then left.

"Are you still living in Boston?" he said.

"It's my home. Yes, Boston's my home," she said, almost as if it didn't seem like home and it appeared doubtful to Jack that it really was *home.*

Then she looked at his business card she still held in her hand. "I'm happy for you Jack that you are doing so well."

"I've been lucky. After the war, I took advantage of the GI Bill, studied engineering at New York University."

She smiled. "I think it's more than luck. You have a gift as an architect to have won so many awards."

All this conversation seemed polite, but he had to know if she felt the way her paintings spoke to him. She didn't commit to answering his question if she loved her husband. He was just about to ask her when the waitress appeared again.

"If you folks don't want anything else, here's the check," she said, and walked away.

"Well…I guess…I should go." As Sarah rose from her seat to leave, Jack reached for her hand, and there was that sweet sensation as when he touched her hand for the first time.

"There's always another plane," he said.

Her hand still in his...this is what she wanted...here it was at last. It appeared they had never lost each other. Then it seemed as if she could feel her father still controlling her, his unforgiving hand reaching out from the grave, pulling her back to the past and she needed to go, leave, suppress her desire as she once did.

Pulling her hand away, Jack rose from his seat. "I have to go," she said and walked away.

Jack stood at the table, watching her image disappear through the doorway. It appeared life had gone on before without her, now it must once again. He paid the check, slipped on his cashmere overcoat lying on the seat next to him, picked up his briefcase, and made his way to the entrance.

Leaving the coffee shop, Sarah didn't hesitate and started to walk away from the entrance until she heard her mother's dying words whispering to her, *Find what makes you happy. Find it, hold onto it. Fill the empty part of your heart.*

With no hesitation, she turned back.

Just outside the coffee shop entrance, Jack saw Sarah standing across the walkway, a smile forming on her face. She couldn't say goodbye, not again, holding in her heart that young soldier she abandoned at the train station too long ago.

She walked slowly toward him. What seemed the

impossible was now hers to embrace. She threw her arms around his neck.

"Oh Jack, I'm not alive without you."

His briefcase fell from his hand onto the floor as he held her. Here was the moment they had longed for and thought would never come. Passing travelers slowed to take notice, amused look on their faces before moving on. It didn't matter to Sarah and Jack. He held her tight as if he was gripping the cockpit wheel of his B-17 bomber where the very moment meant life or death.

Chapter 39

The valet set their luggage on the penthouse floor. It was the suite at the Le Grand Chateau Hotel Sarah and Jack had shared together twenty-three years ago with its balcony overlooking Central Park, and the suite a young soldier was unable to afford. He could have taken her to his posh New York apartment, but nostalgia brought him to the Le Grand Chateau, perhaps to relive the past, or begin anew.

The suite had been beautifully redecorated with summer colors of pink, yellow, and blue. Dozens of red roses stuffed in vases on tables throughout the suite, filled the room with the sweet scent of summer, defying the autumn wind rearing its head outside.

Champagne chilling in a crystal ice bucket sat next to caviar on a table beneath a vase of red roses where petals were scattered across the glass table top. *A soldier who once didn't care for champagne,* she thought. *Jack must have arrange all this when he made a phone call from the airport.*

In the past twenty-three years on her usual shopping trip to New York, Sarah always stayed at the Le Grand Chateau Hotel, but never reserved the 1941 suite. At first she thought it presumptuous of him to assume they would take up where they left off, but it all seemed very natural. After all, they are not strangers. Philip was his son, born out of their love, and she would tell him as she had tried to in the letters she had burned.

Jack paid the valet and then courteously asked Sarah to excuse him to make a brief phone call to his office. As he went to the phone in the bedroom, Sarah sat on the sofa in the living room and waited for him. She could hear his voice coming from the other room that he was going on to Washington and wouldn't be back at the office beforehand.

"Gordon, this is Jack."

"Jack, you'll be pleased to know, the paintings are hung in your office. The spotlights really bring out their brilliancy. You were right, Jack, they're different. You have to see them with the lighting. Absolutely breathtaking."

Jack was pleased, but even more pleased since he had the artist in the other room.

"How did you find them, Jack?"

"Just stumbled upon them."

"The artist's name sounds familiar. Is she the girl you met before the war?" Gordon said.

"Yes."

"She's quite an artist. You never told me about that."

"I didn't know at the time," Jack said.

"After all these years, you're still in love with her. I didn't think any woman could grab a man's heart the way she has yours. Do you think you'll ever see her again?"

"I'll talk to you later?"

"What's going on, Jack?"

"Now is not the time to discuss this." Jack made it clear, besides there was a strong possibility Sarah who was sitting in the adjoining room, could overhear their conversation.

"How'd it go in Philadelphia?" Gordon asked.

"The proposal was accepted for the fifty-two story office building. They were elated with the design, thought it might win the AIA Award."

"Another one of those?"

"Designing is what we like to do, Gordon, and doing it well is what it's all about. Awards are just part of the process." He knew he needed to end the call.

"I won't be returning to the office today, and I can't be reached the rest of the day. Anything comes up, Gordon, I'm sure you can handle it. I'm going directly to Washington tomorrow early afternoon, and back to New York same day on the Northeast Airlines' seven o'clock evening flight. I'll see you then. Goodbye."

He hung up and walked back into the living room. As he apologized to Sarah for the delay, the elevator doors opened to the suite and a boy appeared holding a large box. "Delivery from Saks," the boy told Jack.

Jack took the box and placed a generous tip in the boy's hand. The boy thanked him and cheerfully stepped back on the elevator, a skip in his step and a wide smile slapped on his face as the doors closed.

Jack walked to the sofa and set the box next to Sarah. He opened the box, pulled out a simple, but exquisite black, silk evening dress, and held it up for Sarah to see—

thin straps, low cut, very different than her demure dress of 1941. Size tag—four—still attached. *How did he know?*

She looked around the room again at the roses, champagne and caviar. He truly thought of everything. It appeared she was wondering what other magic he would pull out of his hat. He was even more than the Jack she once knew. He was always self-confident, but now he had a maturity, a sophistication that success had brought him, and a grace to add to his audacious nature.

He handed her the dress.

"For dinner and dancing tonight at the Saint-Veran restaurant," he said.

"How did you do all this?"

"One phone call," he said matter-of-factly.

"Are we reliving the past, lieutenant?"

"We are living the present, remembering the past." Taking her hands in his, he coaxed her from her seat on the sofa.

"How would you like a hot dog?" He wanted to take her in his arms, but he thought he had better move slowly.

"Hot dog…do you think the stand's still there?"

"I know it is."

Chapter 40

Sarah dressed for dinner in the black silk while Jack was gone on an "errand" he had said. When he returned, he had one hand behind his back and a childlike look on his face as if he was hiding something.

"What is this Jack? What are you up to?" She smiled. He had already won her heart long ago. He didn't need to try so hard.

Then, he brought his hand forward in a gesture of surprise.

Tucked in his hand was a small box tied with a red ribbon. He handed it to her, and said, "Because my heart can never tell you how much I love you."

Hidden under the ribbon, the name *Tiffany and Co.* appeared on the box. She glanced at him, wondering what could possibly be inside while he seemed to be anticipating her reaction, a smile of great satisfaction on his face.

Inside was a platinum brooch generously clustered with brilliant diamonds. Besides her wedding ring, engagement ring, and the solitaire diamond Winston gave her on her wedding day she had a few simple pieces of jewelry, handed down through the generations. She never cared to wear them, but perhaps Mary would.

"Oh Jack." She was overwhelmed with his generosity.

"It's the most beautiful piece I've ever seen...but...I can't accept it."

"Why not?"

"It wouldn't be right."

"It's not like you just knew me, Sarah."

She set it back on the velvet interior of the box.

He placed his hand on her arm. "Sarah, please don't deny me this pleasure. It's just something I've wanted to give you since the gardenia corsage. Although this was not compliments of the hotel as the corsage was."

They laughed, reminiscing.

She removed the brooch from its box, walked to the mirror above a side table and pinned it to the black dress just above her left breast, below the thin shoulder strap—galaxy of stars radiant in the night.

"It takes my breath away, Jack." She turned away from the mirror to face him, and he saw the true beauty of it on her dress. But there was no competition. Without question it appeared to him, she outshined the piece.

He looked at his watch. "We have only twenty minutes until our reservation. I'm sorry this errand took so long. Give me fifteen minutes to shower and shave."

While Jack was in the shower, Sarah took the elevator to the lobby to use the house phone to call George. It wouldn't be appropriate to call George from the suite. She would be back before Jack was dressed.

"I've decided to stay another day." Sarah told George.

"I was expecting you home this evening."

"I know George."

"Is everything alright?" he said.

There was a hesitation as if she wanted to say more.

"I'll see you tomorrow evening, George." She hung up.

Chapter 41

The band was setting up on a two-step platform when Sarah and Jack arrived and were seated at their table in the Saint-Veran restaurant. The dance floor was in front of the band and the tables formed a half circle around the dance floor. Nothing had changed.

She had not been to the Saint-Veran restaurant since she was there with Jack. She always had her meals in her room when she came to New York on her annual shopping trip. George never cared to go to New York. He didn't want to leave Boston, except to go to their summer home on Cape Cod. Although she and George had toured Europe twice after the war to educate the children, but that was the extent of their travels.

In a quiet moment, Sarah and Jack sat at their table in the Saint-Veran restaurant and looked at each other. Each wondering, perhaps, how this all happened.

"I still have the farm," he said, breaking the silence between them, knowing she hadn't forgotten his description when they first met. "My folks passed away. My brother was drafted and didn't survive the first wave that landed on Omaha Beach at Normandy. I wanted to bring him home to Iowa, but I think being buried at Normandy among his men, high on that hill above the sandy beach, is what he would have wanted.

"Although the farm had been left dormant for years during the war, my brother and I kept the taxes paid since our mother died. It took all our soldiers' pay through the war years, it meant that much.

"I've expanded the land to five hundred acres. I have a manager who lives there as an overseer. The farm pretty much pays for itself, and most years with a fairly large profit, but that doesn't matter, I'm successful.

"I've kept the old house, but designed and built a large home next to it with lots of floor to ceiling glass to let the sunlight stream in, see the corn growing. The farm is a retreat. I go for harvest mid-September when the corn is ripe and golden, and try to go in the spring for planting, work alongside the field hands. Get away from all this and sweat in the sun, feel the soil beneath my feet and appreciate how hard it is to work a farm, the love of the soil the farmers have. Some semblance of peace you are unable to find anywhere else. I'll always keep the farm. My roots are tied to the cornfields of Iowa. Tilling the soil and harvesting the corn restores my spirit. There's nothing like a farm."

For years, she had often wondered what it would be like to be in his vision of home.

"You have two children," Jack said.

"How did you know?"

The day in the park, he watched her from afar, imprinted in his mind.

"What are their names?" he said.

"Philip and Mary."

"Philip." A distant look came to Jack's eyes, and Sarah wondered why he focused on Philip.

"What are they like?"

"Mary's very studious, serious where Philip is a gentle, kind soul with such energy, finding pleasure in simple things." Sarah watched Jack who nodded as she spoke, appearing to take in with such intensity everything she said. And then he seemed even proud when she added, "Philip entered Harvard law this fall. Mary is in her third year at Yale."

She looked closely at Jack, his thoughts faraway.

"How is it Jack, being what you want?"

"Oh, I don't know. Life just sort of happened for me."

"Happened?"

"Yes, there was the war, and then architecture. But we all have choices."

"I think of it as commitment," she stated.

"But a commitment is a choice. You choose to fulfill the commitment even if it's not what you truly want."

The band's introductory music began and Jack rose from his chair, and reached for her hand.

"Come, let's not waste the night away. I have to remind you, I'm not good at fancy dancing. Slow is best for me." Obviously he remembered saying those words once before."

"No practice?" Sarah said.

"No time during or after the war."

"Slow then. I can manage that."

As Jack led Sarah onto the dance floor, taking her in his arms, he pressed her ever so close to him, wishing that their clothes weren't between them, to know her purity as he once did. He didn't care if she loved George. He sensed it wasn't the same.

A vocalist walked to the microphone, and sang the song from the London nightclub during the war so long ago, the words always reminding him of her...

...After the war is over,
And you're in my arms again,
I'll whisper that I love you,
I just don't know where or when....

Chapter 42

The abrupt way Sarah ended her phone call worried George. Something didn't seem right.

In the backroom of the Le Grand Chateau Hotel, the switchboard operator was busy answering incoming and connecting outgoing calls, plugging cords into the proper slots indicating room numbers on the switchboard.

"Le Grand Chateau Hotel," she said to an incoming call, gripping the mouthpiece pushing it closer to her lips.

George's voice came from the other end.

"Mrs. Minton's room, please."

"One moment please," she said, then checked the list of registered guests to find the room associated with his request. But there was none.

"Sorry sir. A Mrs. Minton is not among our registered hotel guests."

She did say she was staying another night, he thought. *She always stays at the Le Grand Chateau Hotel.*

"Are you sure? Would you check again?" he said.

The hotel manager happened to be in the switchboard room behind the front desk, and heard the operator say Sarah's name. He knew Sarah well. She was a regular at the hotel during her New York shopping trips. He knew Jack too, having dinner at least twice a week at the Saint-Veran restaurant, and generally reserved the penthouse suite for his out-of-town clients. But then, everyone in New York knew of its most prominent architect.

The hotel manager walked over to switchboard operator, leaned down and placed his hand over the operator's mouthpiece, then quietly asked the operator, "Is that a call for Mrs. Minton?"

"Yes, sir," the operator said.

"She's at dinner with Mr. Karsen. Just tell the caller, she's at dinner, and take a message." The hotel was very discreet about their guests' behavior. The hotel manager walked away.

The operator returned to George holding on line. "I'm sorry, sir, Mrs. Minton is at dinner with Mr. Karsen. Would you like to leave a message?"

Karsen. He remembered the day years ago when he found the article and photo of Jack in the Boston newspaper on one of the library side tables The newspaper commentary had touted Jack's success as a highly sought after New York architect. His gut feeling had told him at the time something wasn't right, but dismissed the thought to an unjustified fear. Now the hidden memory surfaced and the fear appeared to become reality.

With no answer from George, the operator repeated, "Sir, would you like to leave a message for Mrs. Minton?"

"No, it won't be necessary." George told the operator and hung up, his hand still clinging to the phone.

Chapter 43

The music flowed through the Saint-Veran restaurant. Guests flooded the dance floor, bumping into each other as Sarah and Jack moved to the fox trot.

"Jack?" Sarah whispered in his ear, and he pulled his cheek away from hers.

"Yes," he smiled.

"Something you said…that you never married. You mean you've never had anyone you cared about?"

"Not enough to say the two words."

"So, there's no one I should be jealous of?"

He laughed.

"Why is everything so wonderful when I'm with you?" she said.

"Maybe because there's no one like me," he joked.

She laughed. Nothing had changed between them, their love was deeper. Years of longing had made it so.

They danced until everyone in the Saint-Veran restaurant had gone, and the band concluded the evening with the popular British song, *Goodnight Sweetheart.*

"That's all for the evening." The band leader said and the band members began storing their instruments in their cases.

As Sarah and Jack walked to their table to grab her wrap lying over a chair, he excused himself.

"I'll be right back." Jack walked across the dance floor toward the band leader, shook his hand, gave him five, one hundred dollar bills, thanked him, and said goodnight to all the members. Then he rejoined Sarah who was waiting for him at the table.

"Very generous of you Jack," she commented.

Jack shrugged and smiled. He was a proponent of hard work and the use of one's own talents to accumulate wealth. He was also generous in sharing the rewards of his hard labors with those who don't expect handouts which he most adamantly believed stifled the human spirit's incentive. And he was doing it for all the men in his crew who couldn't enjoy an evening dancing, because they didn't make it back from the war.

Chapter 44

In silence, Sarah and Jack walked through the Saint-Veran restaurant, across the lobby to the elevator where Jack instructed the elevator operator to take them to the twenty-fifth floor.

On the elevator to the penthouse suite, no word was exchanged between them. At first he stared at her in a way that she felt uneasy. Then he looked away, and there was a silence deader than the silence felt in the officers' club when news came that a pilot was gone.

She placed her hand on his arm, but he didn't respond. He didn't even look at her. She observed the quiet as it appeared he desired.

They reached the entry to the penthouse and while the elevator doors closed behind them, leaving them alone, Sarah removed her wrap, went to the sofa and laid it there. Standing in the subtle moonlight flooding the room through the windows, she turned to him where he stood in the shadows by the elevator doors.

"What's the matter Jack? You haven't said a word since we left the restaurant."

No answer came. Instead he went to a side table, reached for the small lamp and switched on the light. A soft glow fell across the room. Taking off his jacket, he threw it on the chair next to the table. He loosened his tie, unbuttoned his shirt collar, then pulled the tie away tossing it on the chair.

She stood in the silence, watching him. What did this silence mean?

He contemplated pouring a drink from the bar for what he had to say, but since the war, he wasn't much of a drinker. He already had a few too many throughout the evening.

On the elevator, he knew he had to get some things off his chest. It was eating at him, and now, it had reached its boiling point. All this happiness they had this evening could have always been theirs, every day since that summer day of 1941 and he had to know why he was denied it. Why she denied it of herself?

He turned to her, standing nearby, his look hard, his eyes communicating great tension. Suddenly the past ignited itself and came to life.

"Why didn't you come to the train when I left for the war, why didn't you? I waited for you, standing on that railway platform, hoping to see you, and you just sent me a telegram. Convenient. Impersonal. A cold piece of paper." He closed his eyes while shaking his head in disbelief. "I was a soldier going off to war, and you ripped my heart out. I can't believe that time in New York didn't mean anything to you."

It appeared she didn't know how to respond, how to tell him she was fearful of an uncertain future that was not planned for her. A young girl conditioned to living a certain life, bound by tradition soaked with Winston's ideology. But why hurt him again?

She bit her lip and said, "I wanted to be with you."

"Then what could possibly stop you?" His tone was constant, demanding.

She answered him as if it was the only way she knew how. "There was more than just us, Jack."

"Not for me there wasn't. What does this all mean to you now, Sarah? Why are you even here? Are you going to be here for one night and then leave again?"

"I think I should go." She turned to leave, and he rushed before her, leaning his back against the elevator doors, blocking her exit.

He had been climbing straight for heaven since she came back into his life and this time, he wasn't going to crash. The years of pent up anger were not going to get in the way. Oh, how he loved her, and there she stood just as he had envisioned her in his mind all those years. She was his and he was hers and he wasn't going to let her go, even if he could only have one night.

His voice softened, almost pleading. "I thought I'd never see you again, and when I saw you in the airport, it was the release of all the years of hope I held in my heart. Do you know how many times I wished I was the one lying beside you each night? Don't you understand, Sarah, only you can heal my heart."

She placed her hand over his heart and felt it racing. She looked deep into his eyes and found his yearning. When the eyes speak, they reveal the soul.

"Now is what matters, Jack. I can't and I won't leave

you, not this time."

He held her in his arms and confessed: "Deep in my heart I longed for you Sarah. You are life to me. I loved you then…I love you even more now…and I will die loving you."

Desire consuming him, he kissed her with a passion longing to be released, his lips touching her neck while his hands glided across her shoulders, sliding down the thin straps of her dress.

In the heat of the moment, she ripped the buttons from his shirt pulling it away from his chest. Their clothes stripped away in a frantic desperation to fulfill their long awaited need for each other. It was lust, but it was pure, calling on the universe once again to grant them that pleasurable moment of ecstasy when two souls embrace. And each time their need was repeated, it was more pure. The universe had smiled upon them, and it was theirs. Together they were truth. Now and forever.

In their nakedness they lay together, the warmth of their bodies against the soft sheets. They could share every moment of every single day and their hunger would never be satisfied.

He pulled her close to him and when she reached up and kissed his cheek, he smiled. What would her father think now? Jack was new money, not inherited, but acquired by the sweat of his brow—Winston, too proud to turn away from tradition, ironhanded to his last breath.

Thinking of her father brought George to mind. Was it wrong to be with Jack when it was truly right? She was a married woman, but she wasn't ashamed. After all she wasn't being unfaithful. She had belonged to Jack before George ever touched her. Now, she thought, she was her own person, answering only to herself. Free. Free of the old thinking of the Wescotts. Free to follow her heart.

She didn't care what Boston society would say. Time had loosened the chokehold on women. What was unacceptable by society then appeared to be somewhat commonplace now. She didn't want to hurt George. It didn't seem fair to him, but somehow as the years wore on, she had thought that he hadn't been entirely in agreement to an arranged marriage. He too was fulfilling his father's wishes.

Lying beside Jack, she gently brushed the hair from his forehead, her fingers moving down over the curve of his nose, over his lips. She watched his chest rise and fall with each breath, then moved to listened to his heartbeat. *Keep beating, Jack, for me.* She rested her head on his shoulder again, her fingers drawing gentle strokes across his chest, feeling the smoothness of his skin until she touched a scar on his shoulder.

"War wound," he said.

"How did it happen?"

He removed her hand from where she touched the scar, lifted his head and kissed her hand, then laid his head back on the pillow.

"It was a long time ago," he said. *Memories to be forgotten,* he thought, *but refuse to let you forget.*

"You should tell me sometime," she said.

"You really don't want to know."

Chapter 45

In the morning Sarah was awakened by sharp sunlight streaming across her face, invading the room through a crack in the drape. She heard the shower running, and noticed Jack was not lying beside her. She grabbed the pillow next to her and threw it over her face, as she thought, *never too late to find a rainbow*. Then she hummed the tune, "After the war is over, and you're in my arms again," the pillow muffling the sound. If her father was there, she could tell him proudly that Thomas Jefferson, founding father, was an architect and a farmer like Jack. "Those who labor in the earth are the chosen people of God." Jefferson once wrote.

She tossed the pillow back on the soft sheets. In her nakedness, she rose from the bed, and decided to pick up their clothes strewn across the floor they had so hastily removed the night before. When she picked up Jack's silk shirt, and rubbed the softness against her face, breathing in the lingering scent of aftershave—citrus with a whisper of white musk—she felt something in his breast pocket. Slipping her fingers inside, she removed the newspaper clipping, faded with age and stained with dried blood, so fragile, it appeared it would crumble to dust. She opened it to a photo of her wedding day he had kept over his heart since 1941. How he had loved her, more than the depth of a sonnet, a poem or a song could say. To be loved so much was truly a gift. Things were clearer now. Clearer than ever. She must tell Jack about Philip.

When Jack came out of the shower and entered the bedroom, he turned on the radio sitting on a table just outside the bathroom door. He had asked the hotel staff to set the station to music of the '40s. It was obvious that success had not changed him he was still the romantic soldier.

Sarah was still folding their clothes that were lying on the floor when she heard the music. She turned to look at Jack standing a few feet away a towel wrapped around his torso.

She gasped, and then chuckled.

"What?" he smiled.

"Are you the man who made love to me last night? I couldn't see too well in the dark."

He looked around the room to see if there was another man. "I believe I was, so what's so funny?"

"No one who sits behind a desk for a living looks like that. I'd say you look more like a lumberjack."

"I do, do I?" He went to her, picked her up in his arms and carried her to the bed and laid her there. "Well, we'll see how well you love this lumberjack."

There was the warm caressing of their bodies and the rise of fulfillment once again. Then Sarah said, "What else don't I know about you Jack Karsen, like what's hidden in there." She pointed to his heart.

He placed her hand over his heart, "Only you are

there."

"You never loved anyone else?"

"Never touched another woman."

She lifted her head from the pillow, and smiled as she looked into his face. "Something I need to tell you, Jack."

He rose from the bed and slipped on a terry robe lying at the foot of the bed.

He isn't paying attention. Why? She thought.

"Come here," he said gently.

She went to him. As she approached, he opened his robe and when her body touched the warmth of his, he drew the robe about them, enclosing her nakedness with his. She would follow him anywhere for the rest of her life, as sure of it as the sun would rise in the morning and the moon appears in its absence. There was nothing to hold them back.

"Where is this going, Jack? I mean, what are we going to do?"

He touched her hair running his fingers through the long silk strands, a worried look appearing on his face.

She looked into his eyes, searching. "What is it, Jack?"

"All I ever desired in life was to grow old together. I thought it was time for us, that we belong together…but Sarah…you have to go back."

"What?"

"I can't believe I'm saying this."

She pulled away from him and grabbed her robe on the end of the bed, slipped it on, tying the belt in a tight knot at the waist.

He watched her. He didn't want to hurt her. He went to her, and turned her to face him. A tear glistened on her cheek, and he gently wiped it away.

"I don't understand, Jack."

"Don't you see, we were overcome with passion. We're not those two young people anymore. We can't make the summer of 1941 what it should have been. Now we must think more clearly."

"What do you mean?"

"Philip and Mary. How do we justify this to them? They're so young. Don't you realize what this would do to them, their future? All they would feel is their life as they know it would be torn apart. It would cause pain, more than our own suffering. Your family has built a strong heritage, a tradition for generations. You can't tarnish it for them. I didn't understand what it meant to live your kind of life, but I do now. You were right. There was more than just us. There was then, and there is now."

The white dove, soft, pure, was gently clasped in her hand and he was telling her to open her hand, let it fly away.

She turned away from him again.

He placed his hands on her shoulders. "Sarah, look at me," he pleaded, but she refused.

"Sarah, please."

She turned back to him, her eyes heavy with tears. He knew she didn't what to hear the truth. He held her in his arms as he never did before and she cried.

"Sarah, Sarah, my darling," he whispered gently, "there

were times when I thought I could never go on without you. Each day an eternity. I'm more afraid now to be without you than climbing into that cockpit during the war."

"I can't say goodbye, Jack."

"I know, I know," he said tenderly as he held her. "In life we must be brave."

"No…no Jack, I don't care."

"You may not care now, but you will later," he said. "As the years wear on, the regrets will come. Remember, we have what most people never know in a lifetime. These moments will always be ours and no one can take away the summer of 1941."

Chapter 46

From the library window of the Wescott mansion, where Sarah looked out onto Beacon Street, she waited. Waited for George to come home. She thought she had it all planned, what she would say, what words she would form, how she would tell George he was to live without her. That she had given him twenty-three years, now the rest of her life she wanted to give to Jack. And how she would make George understand that Jack was always there from the beginning. That she entered their marriage falsely, robbing George where he believed he was the only one in her life. Solid, dependable George who was devoted to her, but she was obligated to him.

She ran away once, spending years regretting it, but as Jack pointed out to her, there are some things you simply can't turn your back on. Now she must pay the price for having someone go in her place with a telegram in an outstretched hand.

All those years she wanted to be with Jack, loved him from afar, and then when he opened a door she thought was closed forever, it was closed again. It ended just as it ended when it began. She was alone as she was before. Lonely in an unfulfilled marriage. But she still held on to the summer of 1941, she couldn't let go. *There'll be time for us, someday.*

The Bentley pulled into the driveway and Sarah moved closer to the window, pushing away the heavy drape. George always came home like clockwork, at five.

The wind grew stronger, pulling the autumn leaves from the trees, blowing them across the yard. The chauffer opened the back car door and George stepped out into the blustery wind. Holding his hat from being swept away, he walked toward the entry.

Sarah let the drape fall across the window, and turned to face the library door where she knew at any moment George would make his presence known.

The sound of the wind blew wildly through the open entry door, forcing its way into the central hall. Then it was silenced by the closing of the door. There were footsteps across the central hall, then the library door opened and George's image appeared.

Years of stress marked his face. His once thick hair was now thinning, and there was seldom time for leisure or exercise. It would have been difficult for him to live alone. He was not a young man. Almost fifty. He had come to rely on her, especially since the children were gone. Life may have given him much comfort wealth can provide, but with it came more responsibility than he cared to assume. When his father died, George had little knowledge on how to run the day to day Minton business due to Bradford's unwillingness to give up control however small. Then after Winston died, George had assumed the responsibility of two empires. Years of maintaining his professional and social status in Boston society was something George strived for, innate in his being from his upbringing and conditioning. But no one can truly explain why someone is driven the way they are.

"Well, hello dear." George addressed Sarah standing by the window. "The wind is really kicking up out there. Where is Harrington?" George dropped his briefcase on the floor and threw his coat and hat on a nearby chair. The butler usually met him at the entry to take his hat and help remove his coat.

"I let the servants go for the evening." Sarah said.

"Cook too?"

"She left sandwiches."

"A simple fare. That should be interesting," he said. "Seldom do we ever have sandwiches at dinner. Maybe at tea or lunchtime when the children were little. An evening at home, that would be nice. Just the two of us."

He's trying hard to be exceptionally nice. Why? She wondered. *What changed?*

Still standing by the window, Sarah said, "George, I need to tell you about something."

It appeared it might be related to her evening with Jack Karsen, but it was evident he didn't want to think about it—the sordid details.

"Let's not talk just yet. I need to fix myself a drink. Would you like one?"

"Not for me, George."

He loosened his tie as he walked to the table holding the decanters of spirits.

"I was thinking about the trip we talked about, do you

remember?" he said as he poured himself a generous amount of whiskey. He looked at her, but she made no response, just stared at him.

Grabbing the glass, he headed toward the kitchen and she followed.

In the kitchen, he turned on the cook's private television sitting on a counter while Sarah removed a plate of sandwiches from the refrigerator. She turned to George whose eyes were fixed on the television and the evening news.

"George, I need you to listen—"

Suddenly she was interrupted by breaking news, and a fiery mass of burning debris flashed across the television screen. The sound of sirens blared in the background from ambulance trucks racing to what looked like the edge of a runway…

…"We interrupt this broadcast to bring you this breaking news," the reporter said, standing in front of the accident. "Northeast Airlines, 7PM flight, Washington DC National to New York, Flight number 55, has just crashed on landing at La Guardia Airport. The pilot had reported engine trouble moments before. The rescue crew is on the site, but it is reported that of the seventy-six passengers onboard the Douglas DC-6B, all have perished. There are no survivors."…

…A look of shock crossed Sarah's face. She stared at the television screen for a second then she let out a gasp, covering her mouth in disbelief. It was Jack's flight. She remembered overhearing Jack on the hotel phone stating his flight itinerary. He had a meeting in Washington D.C. and returning to New York on the 7PM flight.

The plate fell from her hand, crashing to the floor, pieces flying in all directions.

George, whose eyes were now intensely glued to the television, turned to her when he heard the sound of the plate hitting the floor.

"What is it Sarah?"

She ran from the kitchen, crossing the hall to the library.

He turned off the television and followed her.

Entering the library, George found Sarah sitting on the settee, staring at nothing.

"Did you know someone on that plane?" he said.

She remained silent.

What did her silence mean? Then he looked as if he realized the truth. *Karsen*—his phone call to the hotel.

"Jack Karsen," he said in the silence of the room as if he was pronouncing him dead, and the universe spoke his name for the last time.

She looked up at him, surprised that he knew Jack's name. Then she looked away. A tear fell and she didn't want him to see it. All she could think of, was the silence would never be broken by the sound of Jack's voice, the voice she had waited so long to hear.

"Is there something I need to know, Sarah?" he said, but still no answer came from her. "What could this man give you that I don't provide? You have everything you could possibly want. I've denied you nothing." He stood firmly by the desk where Winston once stood.

"So that's what you think this is all about?" she said, a look of distain on her face.

"What else is there?"

What else is there? She thought. What Winston had denied her.

"I know it wasn't a brief encounter," George said. "How long and to what extent, I don't care. Maybe someday, you'll tell me."

Tell him? The glimpse of divinity? The magic? How does she explain love that reaches to the very depth of one's soul when he was incapable of understanding, knows not how to love completely? She would never tell him, today or any tomorrow. And she would never confess the truth about Philip. She would carry that to her grave.

"You would never understand, George," was her reply.

"What's there to understand?" he said. "We were pledged since you were six and I was twelve. Twenty-three years should mean something."

Why was he pleading? To keep her from a dead man?

She got up from her seat and walked to the fireplace. He followed her, stood behind her as she watched the flames growing high, licking the wood as it crackled, sparks rising through the chimney flue.

He placed his hand on her shoulder, but she didn't

respond, still staring at the fire.

"We can forget this, Sarah, now that it's all behind us," he said indifferently.

Just like Winston who thought saying a few words made everything go away. The past erased. There was just the now and tomorrow. Was Winston winning once again? Would she never be free of him?

Chapter 47

Autumn leaves drifted from branches like snowflakes. Red and gold scattered across the cemetery lawn, nestling against grey headstones. Soon the barren branches would stretch long across a winter sky, and the wind would grow harsh, bringing fall to its knees as the last of autumn relented to a season of white cold.

The sound of dying leaves crunched beneath her feet, as Sarah walked toward Jack's grave. Her eyes were clearly focused on the lone coffin resting above the open grave in the stillness of its surroundings.

When Sarah arrived at the cemetery, the service had concluded, and the mourners were leaving, filing quietly away in all directions. Gordon was among them, wearing a dark overcoat, his red hair now streaked with grey.

He noticed a woman appropriately dressed, black coat and hat, carrying a single red rose, walking across the lawn toward the gravesite a few yards away. Even though it had been years, he thought he recognized her from Jack's description and the 1941 newspaper photo. More than that, she appeared all of what Jack had said—beautiful with an elegance and grace befitting a woman of her stature.

Gordon approached her quietly. "Are you Sarah Wescott?"

She paused to answer, turning her face toward the voice, and to Gordon.

"Yes, I'm Sarah Wescott Minton."

"I feel like an old friend. I'm Gordon Frazer, Jack's business partner," he said, and she recognized his name from Jack's business card: *Karsen, Frazer, AIA*.

"Jack and I had known each other since we were bomber pilots in the war and met during training," he said. "I had to meet the extraordinary woman who held Jack's heart where no other woman could. I feel like I've lived your memory every day myself."

She smiled sadly.

He removed an envelope from the inside pocket of his topcoat, and handed it to her.

"This is the deed to Jack's family farm in Iowa. He signed it over to you after the war, the day he saved it from foreclosure, and asked me to give it to you in the event of his death. He loved that farm, his roots. He wanted you to have his home."

Speechless she stared at the envelope in her hand. Truly, only god knew the intensity of his love.

Gordon started to leave, but turned back. "Your paintings, god's poetry and Summer 1941 are hanging in his office."

She looked up at him in wonderment. So Jack was the anonymous buyer. She was pleased and for a moment, she imagined herself in Iowa, standing on the old wooden porch, the sun bowing low over the cornfield, casting warm shades of gold and red across the sky—young

Philip by her side. *Philip,* she thought. Why didn't she tell Jack when she had the chance? Yet somehow in her heart, she thought he knew.

"Well...goodbye...Sarah," Gordon said solemnly, then walked away.

She now looked ahead at the coffin and continued on toward it. It wasn't difficult to find Jack's obituary in the newspaper. Every major newspaper printed glowing remarks of Jack's accomplishments. Yet, he was first a lowly soldier who survived a brutal war, flying death missions deep into Germany only to meet his end like this. How can life be so kind, yet so cruel?

Alone and in the deadening silence, she stood over the coffin that held Jack's remains. There was no sound of the wind, no bird's song in a tree branch, just a coldness she had never felt before.

She kissed the single red rose she held in her hand, then stepped forward and laid it on the spray of white roses embracing the coffin's lid. She let the tears fall, thinking of what could have been. *How can you love someone so deeply that the world became his single voice?* She wondered. *What magic lies within the human spirit to make it so?* Then the first drop of a soft rainfall fell on the red rose, rolling down a petal to touch the spray of white roses.

As she reluctantly turned to walk away, she paused to look at the envelope in her hand that held the deed to the Iowa farm. Clutching it tightly, she drew it to her heart. Should she tell Philip? Thinking more deeply on it, he was very much in love with a stunning young woman, descendant of a founding father—*old money*. What would this do to him? He was a Westcott and a Minton, that's all he knew and considered by the Boston Brahmin to be an acceptable mate for their offspring, not the son of a farmer. Jack was right. It would have to continue to remain a secret. Her secret.

She slid the envelope into the deep pocket of her long black coat. Then she looked back at the grave one last time, thinking how fortunate they were that their love had been touched by the universe and had seen the face of god. She may belong to the Wescotts, but Jack had her soul.

The black touring car waited on the road beyond the headstones to draw her back to the world from where she came, back to the airport and Boston. Walking through the leaves, the soft rain falling against her shoulders, the sun broke through the heavy clouds, and streamed through the trees, casting a heavenly light across her path.

When she reached the car, the driver opened the door and she slid into the backseat next to George. She didn't look at him, but stared straight ahead. The driver closed the door, and proceeded to take his place in the driver's seat.

Sarah removed her wide brimmed, black hat, pulling the hat pin from the back of the headband. Then pushing the pin back into the headband, she placed the hat on the seat and the empty space between them. Her hair was fashioned smoothly back in a tight twist secured at the base of her head.

George watched her remove her hat, giving him no eye contact, no expression on her face.

"Alright Sarah?" His voice was tainted with little softness. When she didn't respond and continued to stare straight ahead, he thought, *No matter.* Things would return to normal, he was sure of it. What hold this man had on her, death had erased forever.

"Drive on," George instructed the driver.

The car began moving slowly away from the reminder of death that surrounded them, headstones disappearing in the distance, lost in a blink of an eye.

Sarah turned to stare out her side window where the rain pelted hard against the glass. She would never see Jack again, not even the hope of a glimpse somewhere, sometime, somehow. A tear rolled down her cheek…

…*There, there now, dry those tears*…her grandmother's words came clear to her…*No love is ever lost, my dear. He will always be in your heart where your memories live. Now you must let it go…Your inner spirit survives on how your past has conditioned you…Hold your head high. Remember you're a Wescott, descendant of the earliest English Colonists—Blue Blood of Boston.*

Author Biography

Braide Keyland is a multiple award winning producer, screenwriter, director, cinematographer, film editor, and songwriter of independent films.

www.Keyland Productions.com
braidekeyland@yahoo.com
www.imdb.com-braide-keyland

CPSIA information can be obtained
at www.ICGtesting.com
Printed in the USA
BVHW071846151222
654333BV00013B/750

9 780966 475326